CIVIL WAR SAILOR

CIVIL WAR SAILOR

By Irving Werstein

Illustrated by Albert Orbaan

Doubleday & Company, Inc.
Garden City, New York

Gretna School Library

THE JUNGLE SECRET
BONNIE
PONY OF THE SIOUX
NORTH POLE: The Story of Robert E. Peary
THE BLOOD RED BELT
BASEBALL BONUS KID
GREEN LIGHT FOR SANDY
SEA TREASURE
CAROL HEISS: Olympic Queen
KENDALL OF THE COAST GUARD
FOOTBALL FURY
NANCY KIMBALL, NURSE'S AID
RODEO ROUNDUP

Library of Congress Catalog Card Number 62-11436

Copyright © 1962 by Doubleday & Company, Inc.

All Rights Reserved

Printed in the United States of America

Prepared by **B** Rutledge Books

CONTENTS

chapter   page

1   BILLY HARPER   9

2   THE TATTOOED MAN   22

3   BAD NEWS   30

4   BILLY'S MOVE   40

5   UNDER WAY   53

6   TROUBLE BELOW DECK   61

7   THE CAPTAIN'S DECISION   74

8   THE MISSING MEN   85

9   A FUSE IS LIT   95

10   SEA HUNT   106

11   THE BATTLE   119

12   A DREAM COME TRUE   132

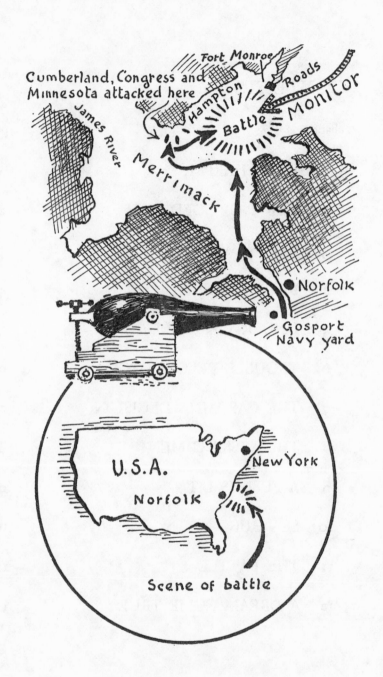

Fort Monroe

Cumberland, Congress and
Minnesota attacked here

Roads

Monitor

Hampton

Battle

James River

Merrimack

Norfolk

Gosport
Navy yard

U.S.A.

New York

Norfolk

Scene of battle

CIVIL WAR SAILOR

Author's Note

In many histories of the Civil War the name of
the ironclad, *Merrimack*, is spelled *Merrimac*.
Actually the ship was named after the Merrimack
River in New Hampshire. Historians confused
this with the name of a small town in Massachu-
setts called Merrimac and the name of the ship
appears that way in many accounts of the famous
sea battle in which it took part.

I

BILLY HARPER

A chill wind that whistled in from the East River made Billy Harper turn up the collar of his navy pea jacket. He blew on his cold fingers and jumped up and down a bit. It was cold standing in that sharp wind at the main gate of the Brooklyn Navy Yard, waiting for customers. Billy was sixteen years old and he was used to long hours in all sorts of weather. He and his shoe-shine box were a well-known sight at the Navy Yard gate from early morning until dusk.

Nearly everyone in the Yard had a warm word for the lean, sandy-haired boy. The workers and sailors at the big naval base liked his wide smile and cheerful manner.

Often, Billy wished that he did not have to shine shoes for a living. He would have liked to go to school with other boys his age, but his mother and father were dead and he had to look after himself.

The stinging wind made Billy's blue eyes water that early morning in March. Winter held on, and in the empty lots near the Navy Yard, dirty gray snows still lay piled in drifts.

"Sure seems that spring will never come," Billy thought. He wished there were a roaring fire at which to warm his hands. But then, remembering the soldiers who were fighting at that very moment, he felt ashamed of complaining about his own lack of comfort.

The war! Billy frowned. Here it was March 7, 1862, and the war had been going on for nearly a year. He recalled the excitement back in April, '61, when the news had come that the Southern soldiers had fired on Fort Sumter, down in Charleston, South Carolina.

"It's war! It's war!" people shouted in the streets.

After many years of bitter feeling between the North and the South, the war had finally come. In Washington, President Lincoln called for 75,000 men to join the Army. The great United States was torn by civil war.

Billy remembered the way it had been for weeks after the war started. The Navy Yard worked around the clock to outfit ships and sign up sailors. How jealous he had been of anyone old enough to join the Navy.

Once, he had tried to join. He was tall for his age and had made out the papers, thinking to fool the officers that he was old enough to join. But the officer who had taken his paper just looked at him and growled, "Go home, sonny! Uncle Sam doesn't need boys to do a man's job! Go home and grow up!" The wise sailor had not been taken in by Billy's height. He guessed the boy was not yet seventeen, the youngest age to sign up in the Navy.

The war dragged on. Billy became used to seeing companies of blue-clad soldiers marching to the Brooklyn docks where they boarded troop ships that carried them south. He had become used to seeing the wounded on their crutches and the many blinded and crippled young soldiers and sailors back from the war.

Billy shivered in the cold. Out on the front lines, thousands of young men were gathered around small campfires, hoping to find warmth. At sea, men stood watch as icy spray froze on decks and ropes. They were fighting the war and he wanted to be with them. Why, in the Army, they had drummer boys who were much younger than he. Some of them were only twelve or thirteen years of age. But the Army was not for him. He dreamed of the sea, of ships and wind, of white foam and blue waters.

The Navy! That was where he belonged. Even as a little boy—only six or seven years old—he remembered how Grandpa Jonas, who had been a sailor on *Old Ironsides* in the War of 1812, told him of tall ships and sea fights. Even now he could hear his mother's scolding voice. "Hush, Pa, you are getting the lad all worked up!"

"Stop that talk, Janey!" Grandpa Jonas always replied in his thundering voice. "This young one has the smell of salt air in his nose! He will grow up to wear navy blues and dance to the tune of the sea or my name is not Jonas Macready!"

After listening to Grandpa Jonas, there were nights Billy had fallen asleep to dream of big ships and cannon shooting flame. Sometimes the old man would walk with him to the top of a hill where they could look out across the bay toward the ocean. Grandpa would speak more softly then as he stared over the water and told Billy of far-off places, of islands with swaying palm trees and shining white sand.

"Aye, lad, aye, but that was long ago," Grandpa Jonas had said with the sadness of old age in his voice.

"That *was* long ago," Billy thought.

Grandpa Jonas was gone now. They were all gone—Mamma and Papa and even the house with the green roof and the garden on that country lane in Brooklyn less than a mile from the Navy Yard.

Billy sighed at the memories of that happier time, then stood up straight. He had no time for the past. There was work to do. He waved his hands and called to the workers who were entering the Navy Yard for the morning shift.

"Shine! Shine! Best shoe shine in town! Only five cents! Shine, sir?"

"I will be back later, Billy!" a carpenter said. "No

sense messing up a fancy shine while I am at work."

"Hey, Billy!" a sailor coming off duty cried. "Over here! Polish my shoes! I have to meet a girl."

Soon, other sailors stationed in the Navy Yard came to Billy. For a while, he even had a line of customers for his services. By the time the noon whistle sounded, the pockets of Billy's pea jacket were heavy with the coins he had earned.

In spite of the cold, he was sweating. He worked hard, rubbing and snapping the polishing cloth to make his customers' shoes take a good shine.

At noon Billy, feeling hungry, walked across the street. A hot-corn peddler had set up his stand. Next to him was a man selling oysters and another who had a little stove on wheels which was filled with glowing coals. On the bed of coals sweet potatoes were roasting. These men appeared every noon time along with the sandwich and butter-cake man. Each had a cry for peddling his wares.

"Hot corn! Hot corn! Come buy my lily-white hot corn so I can go home!" sang the hot-corn peddler.

"Oh, oysters, oh! A dozen for a dime! Buy 'em now! Buy 'em now, and don't waste my time!" the oyster man called in a singing voice.

Billy pushed his way through the workers who now crowded around the carts and stands to buy their lunches. He spent ten cents for a thick roast-beef sandwich and three cents for a mug of steaming coffee. Then he sat down on his shoe-shine kit and began eating.

As he chewed the sandwich, Billy watched the sailor standing guard just inside the Yard gate.

The bluejacket was young, with smooth cheeks. But he made a sharp military figure in his tight blouse, bell-bottomed trousers and pancake-shaped hat. A belt holding cartridges was strapped to his waist. A bayonet in its case hung from his side and on his right shoulder was a rifle.

Billy munched and sipped his coffee and slipped into a daydream in which he was the guard. A Rebel agent tried to slip past him, but he captured the enemy after a hard fight. Then, as President Lincoln was about to pin a medal on him, a voice snapped, "Look alive, lad! How about a shine!"

Startled out of the dream, Billy turned around. "Yes, sir," he said, "I was just having a bit of lunch." He looked up and a wide grin spread across his face.

"Tom!" he cried happily. "Tom! When did you get back from Washington?"

"A few hours ago, on the morning train," Lieutenant Tom Hurst replied. He was a strong-looking young man, twenty-two years old and nearly six feet tall. In the fashion of the day, Tom wore a mustache, which made him seem older. He was dressed in a trim, well-tailored uniform. The two gold-braid stripes which told his rank gleamed on his jacket cuffs.

"Well, Billy, did you look after things while I was away?" he asked.

"Aye, sir!" Billy said, saluting.

Tom grinned as he returned the salute. "At ease, lad. What were you dreaming about when I came up? I stood behind you for two minutes and you didn't even move."

"Oh, I was just thinking, Tom. You know, the same old thing."

"The Navy?"

Billy nodded his head. "The Navy."

"You will be able to join up in another year."

"I don't want to wait that long," Billy cried. "Darn it, Tom, there is a war being fought. A life-and-death war. You know how I feel! I am against slavery and for the Union! I am big and strong for my age. Why, I don't even have a family to raise a fuss! You need sailors— every day there are calls for men to sign up. Why can't I join?"

"Rules, lad. Rules," Tom said, smiling at Billy's words.

Billy pulled off his wool knit cap and flung it on the ground. "Rules! I hate the word!" Then his anger cooled off. He picked up the cap, dusted it off and put it back on his head. "Golly, Tom, I am sorry. But I can't help it. I get so mad!"

"Sure, Billy, I know. Blow off steam, if you must. But the only way you can get into the Navy before you are seventeen is for the Secretary of the Navy to write a special order giving you that right."

"Oh, sure!" Billy cried. "I can see that. Secretary Welles never even heard of me!"

"You will be a sailor yet, lad!" Tom said, clapping Billy on the shoulder. "Now, cheer up, boy. Come on around to the ship this evening. I will be working late."

"Thanks, Tom. I promise I will be there," Billy said. "But why do you have to work at night?"

"Captain Worden wants the ship in sailing trim. We will be leaving very soon."

"For good?" Billy asked.

"Of course not. We will be back. This is our home base—the good old Brooklyn Navy Yard! Now, I have to see the Captain. He will want to hear my report. See you tonight."

"Aye, sir!" Billy laughed. He watched Tom walk through the gate. The guard saluted smartly, bringing his rifle to a sharp present arms.

Billy knew Tom was twenty-two years old. For five years Tom had served on all kinds of naval vessels and had sailed to many strange ports. When the war broke out in April, '61, Tom had been promoted, and now in less than a year, he was a full lieutenant, a Navy officer with the two gold stripes of his rank.

Billy thought about the trip that Tom was about to make. He realized it might be the most important one of Tom's entire life. He was going to sea aboard a ship that was different in design from any other vessel in the U. S. Navy—or any other navy in the world, for that matter.

Looking through bars of the high iron fence around

the Yard, Billy could see Tom's ship now, bobbing gently at anchor. Workers swarmed over her flat deck, bolting heavy iron plates into position. Her wheel house was placed near the stern, and forward of that was a low tower from which poked two heavy guns.

The shape of this odd-looking vessel that had been named the *Monitor* made Billy smile. The workers said she looked just like a "cheese box on a raft."

In spite of her strange design, the *Monitor* was a mighty ship. She had iron sides in a day when ships were made of wood. Since no one had ever built an iron ship before, Billy wondered if the *Monitor* would really hold up when she went to sea.

Her deck was so close to the water line that even the smallest wave washed over it. And her gun tower revolved so that her twin cannon could fire in any direction. According to John Ericsson, the man who invented her, the *Monitor* had more power than any ship on the water.

Billy thought Ericsson was speaking too soon. Most ships still sailed under canvas, although many had steam engines for extra power. Soon enough everyone would know whether the *Monitor* was any good. She was due to join the fleet blocking the southern port of Norfolk, Virginia.

Billy made an unhappy face. When Tom left, he would be lonely—very lonely, for Tom was like an older brother to him, always ready with a helpful word and a smile.

Tom had once told Billy, "I know what it means to

be without parents. I wasn't much older than you when I lost my folks and had to get along by myself, just as you are doing."

At last, the cold day was coming to an end. When the whistle blew for the daytime workers at six o'clock, it was getting dark. Billy packed up his shoe-shine kit and went to the rented room where he lived. It was in a frame house about two blocks from the Navy Yard.

The attic room was small but clean and it cost him only $1.00 a week. Mrs. Dobbins, who rented the room to him, had two sons in the Army. Her husband worked in the Yard mending sails.

Billy took his supper with Mr. and Mrs. Dobbins every night. In return for the meal, he helped with the kitchen tasks. It was past seven by the time he had finished mopping the kitchen floor. Mrs. Dobbins removed her apron and peered at him over the tops of her square eye glasses.

"So, Billy. Another day is ended. Will you be going out this night?" she asked.

"Yes, Mrs. Dobbins, to see Tom aboard the *Monitor*. He will be shoving off soon."

"That Tom Hurst is a fine young man." Mrs. Dobbins shook her head sadly. "What a pity that such as Tom and my boys must fight a war."

"Sure it is, Mrs. Dobbins," Billy said. "But there was no other way."

"You don't have to be telling me the rights and the

wrongs of it, Billy. But that makes war no prettier. Why, if it goes on another year or so, which heaven forbid, you will be in it, too, marching off in soldier blue."

"No, Mrs. Dobbins, not me," Billy laughed, wringing out the mop. "It is the Navy for me. Then maybe I can get to be an officer like Tom."

"You will do it, too, lad!" a warm voice boomed from the kitchen doorway. Fred Dobbins was standing there, puffing on his pipe, his gray hair gleaming like silver in the gaslight. "Aye, you will do it, what with the practice you are getting here for washing decks."

"Takes more than swinging a mop to become a Navy officer," Billy smiled.

"Aye, lad. That it does," Fred Dobbins agreed. "But the mop is a start. I will bet Commander Farragut himself mopped a few decks in his day."

"Hush, Fred. Stop teasing the boy," Mrs. Dobbins scolded gently.

"I am not teasing him, Mollie. I am simply stating the facts. He will be the finest sailor in the fleet if he keeps working with that mop." Fred grinned and winked at Billy.

"Pay no heed to this husband of mine and run along, Billy," Mrs. Dobbins said. "Say hello to Lieutenant Tom for us."

Soon, Billy was at the Yard gate. The guard on duty waved him past and Billy walked quickly to the Monitor's dock. At this hour, the huge Navy Yard was quiet. No hammers thudded, no metal rang. The silence was broken by the lapping waves and the guard's steps; it was so still that Billy could hear the ships creaking at anchor as they rolled with the current.

He looked around at the *Monitor* and paused, a bit puzzled. A gas street lamp cast a pale glow in the darkness and shone down on the steps leading up to the ship.

A guard was usually posted there, but Billy could see no one. He thought it strange, and as he started to go aboard and tell Tom, he heard a groan from the deep shadows near a storage shed at the end of the dock.

Billy ran to the spot and stumbled over someone lying on the planks. It was the ship's guard and there was blood on his head. The sailor had been knocked out by a blow. Billy opened his mouth to shout for help when he saw a movement aboard the *Monitor*. He went closer and saw a man in overalls kneeling on the iron plates. The man reached into a bag that stood beside him and took out a glass jar filled with liquid.

"What in the world is he doing?" Billy thought.

Suddenly the man stood up, pulled open a door and flung the jar inside the ship. Billy heard glass shatter and the "pop!" of something exploding. Immediately, tongues of flame were dancing out of the door. There was a strong odor of sulphur, as well.

Before Billy could move, the man threw another, and more flames leaped out. The boy paused only a few seconds.

"Fire! Fire!" he shouted, and ran toward the man, who was fleeing from the ship. For a moment, Billy wondered if Tom were trapped in the flames below. Then there was no time to think. The man raced by him and Billy threw himself forward. He grabbed the man's legs and sent him crashing to the rough deck planks.

2

THE TATTOOED MAN

For a moment, the man Billy had tripped did not move, and the boy hoped that the fall to the dock had knocked him out. But suddenly the man began kicking and moving about, to shake Billy loose.

They fought for a few seconds until the man broke free and scrambled to his feet. He aimed a kick at Billy's head and the heavy shoe just missed as Billy ducked.

The man turned and ran; he was fast for his strong build. Billy looked quickly about and saw men rushing toward the blazing *Monitor* as fire bells clanged.

"Help! Help!" Billy yelled. "Help! Over here!" But his shouts were not heard in all the noise and disorder. A hose cart was being dragged to the fire and he heard the men shouting, "Pull! Pull!" as they hauled on the tug ropes.

A bucket line had been hastily formed by the crews of the ships anchored near the *Monitor*. The line reached from the river to the deck of the iron ship. Steam hissed up from the hot plates as the water was poured on them.

Billy wanted to help fight the flames and learn what had happened to Tom. But he had another, more important job—to catch the man who had set the fire.

He darted out in the direction the man had fled. That end of the Yard was almost empty. It was an area of tool sheds and supply shacks which went to the very edge of the river. A wooden walk ran between the buildings and the river bank. Street lamps gave off a yellow gleam.

Running hard, Billy caught sight of the man as he sped under a street lamp. Taking a deep breath, Billy ran even more swiftly. His feet pounded on the boards. Up ahead, the man he was chasing paused to look back.

About a hundred yards farther on stood the high iron fence that surrounded the Yard. Once over that, the man would be in the clear. To Billy's surprise, the man stopped dead and turned to face him, waiting under the light. For the first time, Billy saw that a sailor's handkerchief now masked the lower half of the man's face. A knit cap, pulled low, further hid his features.

"Stay where you are, boy!" the man called in a hoarse voice. "I don't want to hurt you, shoe-shine boy!"

"Why, he knows me," Billy thought in surprise. "He

must have passed me a hundred times, going in and out of the Yard. He could be one of my customers for all I can tell. He is dressed like any of the workers."

"Did you hear me, kid?" the man asked.

"I heard, mister. I heard. Listen to me, now. You don't have a chance. They are coming right behind me. You were seen running away," Billy said, hoping to fool the man, hoping and praying that a guard would appear.

"Don't make me laugh. You were the only one who saw me—and even you didn't see my face. But I don't like to leave traces. Now beat it. Walk away and forget all about me, or else . . ." There was such warning in his voice that Billy felt a shiver of terror.

He glanced about quickly, looking for someone, anyone who could help him. He saw only the empty darkness, but out of a corner of his eye he did see a pile of scrap lumber which stood off to one side, only a few yards away. With a sudden move, Billy ran to the pile of wood, reached down and grabbed up a stout stick. He felt better now, having a weapon, but his throat was tight as ever with fear.

"Ah, so that is how you want to play, is it?" the man said. "You are going to be the hero, are you?"

"I saw what you did! I saw you set fire to the *Monitor!* Do you think I will let you escape if I can help it? My best friend was in that ship. For all I know, he might be dead. You are going to pay for that!" Billy was shouting, his voice shrill with fright and anger.

"You have had your chance, boy," the man said. He reached into his pocket and whipped out a spring-blade knife. The blade clicked open, shining in the gaslight. The man came toward him, waving the blade back and forth. "It isn't too late," he said. "Don't be a fool!"

Billy stared at the flashing steel, at the big hand and the fingers wrapped around the handle. He saw clearly, in the glow of the lamp, a design, colored in ink, on the back of the hand—a horse with a flying mane, rearing up on its hind legs. Billy knew many sailors whose hands and arms carried this kind of drawing. Tattoos, they were called.

Far behind him, on the *Monitor's* deck, were all the sailors Billy needed for help. He wanted to scream, "Here! Come here! I have the man who did it!" But he forced himself to keep silent. No voice could be heard over the racket made by the bells, the shouts and the wheels of fire engines being drawn to the scene over the stone pavement.

There was only one course for him to take. He had to hold this man no matter what happened. With his fingers tight on the stick, he moved forward slowly.

Now the man was quite close. He held the knife low

"All right, sonny. The door is closed for good," he said in a hoarse voice.

Billy's gaze fastened on the knife, on the tattoo mark— the wild horse pawing the air. He gripped the stick and braced himself to strike a blow.

He swung with all his strength, bringing the wood down full force on the man's fingers. There was a howl of pain and the knife fell to the boards. Billy darted in and sent the knife sliding away with a kick.

The man shouted a curse and leaped at Billy. The boy struck again with the stick, but this time he missed. An iron grasp closed around his wrist, and though he fought hard, his strength did not match the man's.

Billy punched with his free hand but his blows did not change the hold that was crushing his wrist. After a few cruel seconds, his nerveless fingers opened and dropped the stick.

"Now, bright boy," the man growled. He seized Billy by the front of the shirt and drew back his fist. But the boy had been in a hundred street fights—he had been forced to battle for his place at the Navy Yard gate scores of times. It was the best spot for blocks around and every shoe-shine boy wanted it for himself. From these fights Billy had learned all the tricks of rough-and-tumble fighting.

As the man grabbed him, Billy kicked out. The point of his heavy shoe caught the man on the shin. The man let Billy go, grabbed the injured leg with both hands and hopped up and down on one foot, bellowing his hurt.

Billy scooped up his stick again, but before he could use it, the man recovered and threw him down hard on the wooden walk.

"I warned you, right enough," the man growled. "Now you will be out of my way for good." Slinging Billy across one shoulder, he stepped to the river edge and shoved him over the bank. Billy tumbled limply into the water with a splash and was swept away by the swift current.

Glancing off toward the *Monitor*, the man shook his fist. "I will fix that iron tub yet!" he said. He found the clasp knife, snapped it shut, and pushing it back into his pocket, walked off into the darkness. As he headed for the fence, he took the handkerchief off his face and walked on as though he did not have a care in the world.

The shock of hitting the water brought Billy completely to his senses. He gulped for air as he sank beneath the surface, weighted down by the pea jacket and thick-soled shoes. He fought to the top, moving arms and legs to keep his head out of the water. The river was swift moving and Billy was pulled out to the center of the stream.

He ducked under and tugged at his laces to free himself of the heavy shoes. At last he managed to shake them loose. He worked himself out of the pea jacket and then started swimming toward shore. From the middle of the stream, he could see the buildings of the Navy Yard and the ships anchored there.

The water was cold, far colder than Billy could stand. After only a few minutes in the river, he felt stiff, and an icy chill ran through him. He forced his arms and legs to beat the water. He seemed to be getting nowhere against the current, which was carrying him to the open sea. He fought hard to reach the shore on the Yard side of the river, but the current pulled him toward the other side. Billy floated past the *Monitor* dock and had a quick view of people rushing about. As he went by, Billy shouted for help. No one heard.

"It is no use," he thought. Suddenly, he was very tired. He felt himself slipping down into darkness. Then, just as he was about to go under, he was thrown by the current against something firm and hard.

With great effort, Billy reached out. His fingers closed on stones and mud, on firm earth. He was up against a narrow bar of land that pushed into the river from the shore line. Inch by inch, Billy pulled himself out until only his legs were still in the river.

He dragged himself farther onto the bar and was on land at last. He managed to roll over on his back. He saw the stars, which twinkled in the sky like thousands of eyes winking at him. He was alone with the stars and the lights in the houses along the New York shore, and the river slapping against the strip of land.

3

BAD NEWS

Billy had no idea how long he had been lying on the sand bar. He gathered the strength to stand up, but he was so weak that he hardly managed to stay on his feet. His teeth chattered and he was not able to stop shivering. The wet clothes he wore stuck to his skin and every gust of wind cut through him like a sharp knife.

He looked about for some mark which would tell him just where he was. He saw the outline of a church steeple a few blocks away, and some distance up the stream he could see the masts of anchored ships. He forced himself to think. He remembered with effort that the Dobbinses' house in which he lived was close to the nearby church.

The ships' masts to the north meant that the current

had carried him below the Navy Yard. There was a point of land that stabbed into the river several hundred yards south of the base, he recalled.

He was only four blocks from home. "Four blocks," he thought. "It might as well be four miles." He took a step forward and almost fell, but he kept on going; he felt that if he remained in this place he would freeze to death.

He dragged forward, keeping his eyes on the church steeple, using it as a beacon. Several times he stumbled and went down on hands and knees. But he pushed himself up again and moved ahead by fits and starts.

At last, he reached the familiar tree-lined block where the Dobbinses' house was. There were lights in the parlor window and he thought this odd, as Mr. and Mrs. Dobbins always went to bed early.

He went up the porch steps and held on to the railing, gasping for breath. The entrance door was pulled open from the inside. Billy saw Mr. and Mrs. Dobbins standing in the doorway and behind them, a tall man, wearing a Navy officer's uniform. He blinked to clear his vision; the three faces swam before him. He knew the Dobbinses, but could not quite see the face of the third man.

"Billy!" Mrs. Dobbins cried out.

"It's me," Billy said. He was afraid to let go of the railing. He felt his legs buckling under him.

Mr. Dobbins and the officer pushed to his side. The officer's face came into range. "Tom!" Billy said. "You are all right. You got away from the fire!"

"Never mind that," Tom said. "Come inside." Mr. Dobbins and Tom helped Billy into the parlor and Mrs. Dobbins rushed after them.

"Sakes alive! That poor boy is soaking wet!" Mrs. Dobbins exclaimed. "Fred, rush him upstairs to bed and get those wet clothes off him. I will make him some hot, strong tea."

"Aye, Mollie. And the way the lad looks I had better fetch the doctor," Fred Dobbins said.

"I know where he lives," Tom Hurst said. "Let me get the doctor. You take care of Billy."

Fred Dobbins half carried Billy to his room. He peeled the dripping clothes off the boy, dried him with a huge bath towel and put him to bed under thick, warm blankets.

Soon Mollie Dobbins came in with a mug of strong, steaming tea. "Here, lad, drink this. It will take away the chill."

Billy sipped the hot tea and felt its warmth spread through him. He was falling asleep when Tom entered with the doctor, a short, fat man with a full beard and eyes that peered through thick glasses.

The fierce little doctor pointed to the door. "Out! Everybody, outside! I will examine my patient now," he said, opening his black leather bag.

"If you need anything, Doctor, I will be waiting in the hall," Mrs. Dobbins said.

"Madam, all I need is to be alone now with my patient!"

A moment later, Tom and the Dobbinses were in the hall. Tom stared at the door of Billy's bedroom.

"I hope that boy is all right. He seemed in bad shape, didn't he?" Tom asked.

"Aye, that he did," Fred Dobbins replied, shaking his head. "I wonder what happened to him?"

33

Gretna School Library

"Land sakes, Fred, does it matter? The poor lad has probably caught a terrible cold or worse, out in this chill night and soaked to the skin!" Mollie Dobbins fumbled in her apron and found a handkerchief. A sob choked off her words and she wiped her eyes.

"There, there, Mollie," said Fred, putting his arm around her shoulder. "Don't get yourself upset. The boy is here and in good hands. The doctor may be grouchy, but he is a very good doctor. Now, there is nothing we can do but wait to hear what he has to say."

Some time later, the doctor came out of the room and faced the three distressed people in the hall. "Well? What are you all looking so sad about? That boy in there has the strength of an ox! Do you think a little swim in the river can hurt him?"

"Then he is all right?" Mrs. Dobbins cried.

"He will be, after a good rest," the doctor said. "I gave him a powder to make sure he will sleep. But he wants to see you before taking it."

"May we go in, Doctor?" Tom asked.

"Go right ahead. Just don't stay too long." The doctor frowned at Tom and the Dobbinses. "Now I am going home. Maybe I can get a little sleep myself. Good night!" A moment later the door closed behind him.

"Shall we go in to see Billy?" Tom suggested.

They all entered the room. Billy grinned at them from his pillow. "Tom! What are you doing here?"

"I was waiting for you to come home. Mr. Dobbins came down to the Yard about midnight, worried that you were out so late."

"It wasn't like you, boy," Dobbins said. "And with the fire engines and all the excitement at the Yard, I went to see for myself whether anything had happened to you."

"I was worried, too," Tom said. "You never showed up at the ship, so when Mr. Dobbins came down looking for you, I decided to go home with him and wait for word from you."

35

"I had quite a time, I can tell you," Billy said. He paused, and took a deep breath. "I am lucky to be alive and back home."

"What happened?" Tom asked.

"First, I want to know how much damage was done to the *Monitor*," Billy said.

"There was no serious damage," Tom assured him. "I was in the passage when the fire started and I dumped a few buckets of sand on the flames. Then the firemen came and the fire itself was over in a few minutes."

"Were you hurt?" Billy asked.

"Of course not," Tom replied. "Now can you tell us your story?"

Billy told them everything—how he had found the guard beaten, how he had chased the man with the tattoo mark, and finally, how he had ended up in the river.

Tom and the Dobbinses listened with great attention. Once or twice, Tom asked a question, and when Billy had finished, Tom nodded his head seriously.

"All this adds up. We were warned by the secret service that Rebel agents would try to keep the *Monitor* from sailing. But it takes more than Greek fire to stop her," he said.

"Greek fire? What is that, Tom?" Billy asked.

"It is a mixture of liquid which bursts into flames on contact with air," Tom explained. "It is called Greek fire because the ancient Greeks discovered that such a combination burned quickly. They used it against enemy ships or houses."

"Mollie," Fred Dobbins muttered, "maybe we had better leave Tom and Billy alone. It is not for us to be listening to Navy business."

"Now you are using your head," Mollie Dobbins declared. "Good night, Billy. If there is anything you might be wanting, just call out. And good night to you, Lieutenant. You will excuse us?"

"Of course. I am not going to be much longer and I know the way out, so don't bother about me," Tom said.

The Dobbinses left the room. Billy yawned and blinked his eyes. "I will not need those powders the doctor left. I could sleep for a month."

"Just a few more questions, lad. Do you think you would know the man again?"

"I never saw his face, Tom. But I did hear him speak. I well remember that voice of his. And then, there is that mark on his hand! If I live to be a hundred, I won't forget it."

Tom stroked his mustache. "The mark is a good lead, all right. There can't be too many men with a rearing horse design like that."

Billy yawned again. "Golly, Tom, my eyes are like lead weights. I'm sorry."

Tom pulled out his pocket watch and glanced at it. "Nearly three o'clock in the morning. High time I shoved off. Good night, lad."

"'Night, Tom," Billy said.

"Turn off the light," Tom ordered. Billy was reaching up toward the gas light when they heard the hoof beats of a galloping horse on the stones below.

Billy sat up, eyes wide. "Somebody is in a big hurry!"

Tom went to the window. "He is stopping here! Why, it is Captain Worden's messenger!"

"Captain Worden? The commander of the *Monitor?*" Billy asked.

"Yes," Tom said.

There were heavy footsteps on the porch and Tom and Billy heard knocking at the door. "Lieutenant Hurst! Are you there, sir?" a man called.

Tom leaned out the window. "Up here, Martinson, what is it?"

"Captain sent me to round up all the officers. I am afraid there is bad news!" Martinson said.

"The ship?" Tom asked.

"No, sir. The *Monitor* is all shipshape."

"Then what is it?"

"A Rebel iron ship sailed out of Norfolk this morning and sank three of our vessels. Captain Worden has all the details. Please report to the ship as quickly as possible, sir," Martinson said. He ran down the porch steps, jumped into the saddle and galloped off at full speed.

"A Rebel iron ship!" Billy exclaimed. "I didn't know they had one!"

"We have known they were building such a ship,"

Tom said, tugging at his mustache. "That is why we were rushing to complete the *Monitor*. You see, when the Rebels captured Norfolk they raised one of the ships our men had sunk."

"You mean the *Merrimack?*" Billy asked.

"That's right. They named her the *Virginia*, covered her with sheet iron, fitted an iron ram to her bow and mounted ten guns on her deck."

"Ten guns!" Billy gulped.

"Yes. She is the most deadly ship on the water—and all that keeps her from destroying the Union Navy is the *Monitor!*"

"But the *Monitor* has only two guns!" All thoughts of sleep left Billy as he jumped out of bed. "Tom! What are they going to do?"

"We will sail as soon as we can and try to catch up with the *Merrimack*." He paused and smiled. "Don't worry about our two guns. They will be a match for the *Merrimack*. Remember, we are trained sailors. Well, I have to go. Take it easy, lad."

With a wave of his hand, Tom left the room, ran down the stairs and went out of the house.

Billy lay down on the bed. Ten guns against two! The *Merrimack* would smash the *Monitor* to splinters in a battle.

"We don't have a chance against a monster like that," he whispered. "We don't have a chance!"

4

BILLY'S MOVE

Just before he awoke the next morning, Billy had a frightening dream. There were sounds which came from people he could not see. One word was said over and over, pushing through the thick curtain of sleep into his mind. "Extra! Extra!" he heard the voices sing out. He dreamed of a wrecked ship, drifting and sinking in a calm sea. Sailors floated about, hanging on to pieces of wood.

They were waving their arms and yelling in chorus. To Billy it sounded as though they were shouting "Extra! Extra!"

Then the scene suddenly changed. He saw the *Monitor* sailing past, smoke and flames pouring out. Men were jumping from the ship into the ocean. Some ran about on deck, their clothes on fire. Billy saw Tom run from the smoking ship. He was outlined in fire, wrapped in flames. Billy tried to reach out and help Tom, but he could do nothing. At last, crazy with pain, Tom threw himself into the sea and before he disappeared under the waves, screamed, "Extra!"

Billy sat upright in bed. He was trembling, and it took several moments for him to realize that he had been dreaming all this horror. With a shiver of relief, Billy swung his legs off the bed and sat on the edge of it, blinking a bit in the bright sunshine that was coming in his window.

Down below, in the street, he heard the voice from his dream calling, "Extra!" Now Billy was sure he heard right: a boy selling newspapers was shouting "Extra!" Other voices took up the shout.

"Extra! Extra! Read all about it!" Boys were selling their papers from one end of the street to the other.

Billy ran to the window and leaned out. He saw men in work clothes, women, school children in groups around each boy, grabbing up the sheets as quickly as he handed them out. He spotted a paper boy he knew standing just under the window.

"Corky!" he called. "Corky, up here! It is Billy Harper!"

"Hey, Billy!" the paper boy exclaimed. "I hear you took a swim in the river last night. How come? It isn't Saturday!"

"Don't be so smart, Corky. Why are you yelling your fool head off?"

"The Rebels are kicking up a storm down Norfolk way. Here, read this!" Corky folded a newspaper and flipped it at Billy, who made a neat catch.

"Thanks. I owe you a penny," Billy said.

"Forget it! My treat!" Corky shouted back over his shoulder. He trotted out of sight waving a paper over his head and crying, "Read all about it!"

Billy opened the paper. Big black words stood out across the top.

REBEL VICTORY AT SEA!
ENEMY IRONSIDES SINKS
THREE OF OUR SHIPS!

Somehow, reading the story gave Billy an even worse shock than hearing it as he had from Tom. The facts were all there. The *Merrimack* had steamed out against the Union vessels and, before she was done, had sunk or grounded three first-class fighting ships: the *Congress*, the *Cumberland* and the *Minnesota*. The rest of the Northern fleet had fled to sea where the *Merrimack* could not follow. Although the wooden ships had fought

hard, shells from their heaviest guns only bounced off the *Merrimack's* iron sides. No one could tell what disasters faced the Union unless the *Merrimack* could be stopped.

Billy tossed the paper aside and sat on his bed. What he had read troubled him greatly. The news story had made no mention of the *Monitor*, but he knew she was going to be thrown into the struggle against the *Merrimack*. Tom and all the others, all the brave men he knew, were soon to be sent into a terrible battle.

Tom was more than his friend. The officer was like an older brother. Fred and Mollie Dobbins were good to Billy, but he felt that they could never take the place of his own father and mother. With Tom it was different. He and Tom were bound together by a certain understanding, for Tom was also without parents.

Sitting there in his little room, Billy remembered the time before the terrible night when his parents had died. He shut out the memory of the fire that had destroyed the Harper cottage on one of Brooklyn's tree-lined streets —a tragedy through which he alone had lived. Instead, he thought of his father, Dan Harper, a big man with powerful shoulders and arms. It needed strength to swing a blacksmith's sledge all day, and Dan Harper had strength to spare.

But for all his size, the blacksmith was a gentle man. Billy recalled the Sunday walks with his father, wandering along the banks of the East River.

44

Sometimes Dan would hire a horse and buggy for a long drive in the country, and they would take a picnic lunch. Sometimes they swam in the Hudson River or hiked along the wooded trails that lined Manhattan's western shore.

And Billy thought of his mother: pretty Jane Harper with the sparkling eyes and gay laughter; they laughed a lot together, all three. It had been a happy time. Now the laughter was stilled, and Billy had been a lonely boy these past three years.

If Tom left, if there was a battle, if the *Monitor* was destroyed . . . The boy made an effort to drive away these dismal thoughts.

A knock sounded on his door.

"Yes?" Billy asked. "Who is there?"

"Mrs. Dobbins, Billy. Would you like me to bring your breakfast?"

"No, thanks. I will be downstairs in a minute," he said. "I have to get to work. I am late enough now." He jumped up and started to get dressed.

"Billy, the doctor said you must rest!" Mrs. Dobbins demanded through the door.

"I feel fine. Really I do," Billy said, hurrying into his clothes.

A few minutes later, he was seated at the big, round table in the Dobbinses' kitchen. Mrs. Dobbins fussed at the coal stove, making pancakes, as Fred Dobbins stamped in from the back yard with an arm full of wood

45

which he set down in the wood box behind the door.

"You are looking mighty bright for a lad who gave us such a scare last night," Fred grinned.

"Oh, I feel fine, sir," Billy said.

"That silly young man thinks he is going to work this morning," Mollie broke in, turning away from the stove to stare at her husband.

Fred dropped into his chair without answering his wife. He reached for the coffee pot and poured himself a cup. He then filled Billy's mug.

"Did you hear me, Fred?" his wife asked.

"I heard, Mollie. What do you figure we two can do about it?"

"Stop him, that's what! Why, the lad has been through an awful accident."

"Now, Mollie!" Fred smiled, "Billy knows how he feels better than we do. Are you fit, lad?"

"Yes, sir. I am all right. Really I am," Billy said. "I must go to work or I may lose my spot at the gate."

"That would be a shame after the way you had to fight for it," Fred Dobbins said.

"Very well," Mrs. Dobbins said, "but I will tell you this. Billy does not stir out of the house until he has a stack of pancakes. He is not going to gulp and run this morning!"

Billy set down his shoe-shine kit at his regular place near the Navy Yard gate an hour later than usual. He had never seen so much activity in the Yard. Messengers on horseback galloped back and forth with orders. High-ranking Navy officers were moving about. He saw Commander Hiram Paulding in a lively conversation with Captain John Worden of the *Monitor* and a number of other officers.

Wagons loaded with all sorts of supplies rolled through the main entrance in a steady stream. There were butchers' wagons carrying sides of beef, grocery carts piled high with boxes of tinned foods, flour, coffee, bags of sugar and crates of eggs; the procession seemed endless. Horses pressed side to side as their drivers tried to thread through the traffic. Whips cracked like pistol shots and a sweating, red-faced sailor bellowed in anger as he tried to straighten out the traffic jam that blocked all the roads inside the Yard.

Billy saw the *Monitor* riding quietly at anchor. Crowds of workers gathered on her deck. They were each busy at a particular task. Billy had never heard such a hammering as that which rose from the *Monitor*. The workers were putting the finishing touches on the vessel and repairing the damage caused by the fire.

In the midst of all the banging, dock workers were taking the boxes from the wagons and piling the goods to stock the iron ship. Cases of food stood next to barrels of gun powder in what seemed like a complete mix-up. But Billy knew that when the time came, everything would be in its proper place, and the *Monitor* would sail, trim and in perfect shape for the voyage.

He grabbed hold of the bars of the iron fence and searched for Tom in the crowd around the ship. At last he saw his friend on the deck, moving among the workers, kneeling to inspect some particular box, patting a man on the shoulder. Soon, Tom came down to the dock to join Captain Worden and the other officers of the ship. Billy watched the men; they looked serious and worried as they talked. After a few minutes, the officers saluted the Captain and the conversation broke up.

The officers moved off to their several posts. A sailor appeared on the deck of the *Monitor* and blew on a bugle the sharp notes of "Assembly!" Within minutes, men of the *Monitor's* crew came running from the long white building near the dock. A sailor whom Billy knew, Officer Ed Healey, walked past.

"What is the deal, Ed?" Billy asked the sailor.

"Are you fooling, Billy? You have eyes. The *Monitor* is going to sail on the afternoon tide." Turning away, Healey shouted at the sailors, "Look alive there! Shake a leg!"

Billy leaned against the fence. He had known that preparations were being made for the *Monitor* to leave. But he had been able to pretend this was not the case. Even after seeing all the boxes and the last-minute rush aboard the iron ship, Billy could still refuse to believe the ship was really about to leave.

Now Billy had heard it from Officer Healey, and he

could no longer pretend that nothing would happen. The *Monitor* was leaving on the afternoon tide with her officers and crew. She was setting forth to battle the monster *Merrimack*, and Billy well knew that she might be sunk. All those brave men might soon be dead, wounded or taken prisoner. Billy knew then that he had to see Tom before the ship sailed.

He packed up his shoe-shine kit and took it to the gate, where a tall young sailor stood guard. "Hello, Billy," the sailor said, leaning on his rifle. "Now, isn't that a stew cooking down Norfolk way?"

"Sure is." Billy nodded. He placed the shoe-shine box in the guard's booth. "Mind if I leave this for a while?"

"Never have before." The sailor grinned.

"Pete, will you do me another favor?" Billy asked.

"That depends. If you need more than a dollar, I can't help out," Pete said.

"It is not money. There is an officer on the *Monitor* I want to see right away."

"Oh, I get it! Sorry, lad. Orders are orders. Nobody comes in without a pass. They have made that a firm rule since that Rebel tried to burn the *Monitor*."

"Pete, you know I am not a Rebel. Be a real friend and let me pass," Billy pleaded.

"Who is this officer you are so determined to see?"

"Tom Hurst."

"Lieutenant Hurst!" Pete exclaimed. "Well, why in thunder didn't you say so? He is your friend?"

49

"Yes, he is," Billy replied.

"Okay. I reckon you aren't a spy. At least you don't look like one to me. Now, if you were to scoot past while I was studying those clouds up yonder, I couldn't help that, could I?" Pete said, winking.

"Thanks, Pete," Billy whispered as he dashed by the guard, who was looking up at the sky.

In a few moments, Billy was standing near the *Monitor's* dock. Up close, the ship did not seem so small. She was 170 feet long and her wheel house stood twenty-five feet high. The huge guns, which would fire shells eleven inches long, poked out of the gun tower.

The work gangs were busy hauling materials aboard. Men pushed handcarts piled high with crates of food and cases of shells up on deck. Crewmen put the cargo in slings and nets. Many hands worked the machines which lowered the goods into the inside of the ship.

Billy found Tom at the forward hatch where the shells for the cannon were stored.

"Billy!" he cried. "I was just thinking about you. How are you?"

"All right, I guess."

Tom patted him on the shoulder. "Now, now, don't sound so gloomy."

"Golly, Tom, that is the way I feel. You will be sailing in a couple of hours, and . . ."

"And what?"

"I don't think this tub has a chance!" Billy said.

50

Tom eyed him closely. "Is that what really is bothering you?"

"No! I am going to miss you, Tom! I want to go along!"

"You can't, Billy. Now be a good lad and clear out. There is much to be done before we steam away," Tom said. He thrust out his hand. "Don't worry, we will sink the *Merrimack!*"

"Sure you will, Tom. You take care of yourself. Real good care."

Billy and Tom shook hands. Then the boy turned and fled from the ship. When he looked around, Tom had

gone below decks. For a while, Billy waited around, watching the loading. All at once, he saw a huge piece of folded canvas lying on the dock, ready to be put aboard the ship.

Without stopping to think, Billy stepped to the canvas. No one was looking! Quietly, he lay down and crawled between its folds. He stayed there, not making a sound. Then, as ropes were lashed around the canvas, Billy almost cried out, to tell them he was inside. But he kept silent.

A rough voice called, "All secure? Haul away!"

Billy felt the canvas being lifted up into the air. He was swaying higher and higher and then, just as quickly, he was dropping, down, down, until the canvas that hid him landed with a thud that shook him. He was aboard, down deep in the ship, and if he remained out of sight until she sailed, he would be riding toward the greatest adventure of his life.

"And, if we do come to grips with the *Merrimack*, probably my last adventure as well," he thought, in a moment of fear, trembling in his hiding place.

5

UNDER WAY

Billy quickly discovered that being lifted aboard the *Monitor* was easier than lying curled up beneath the folds of canvas. Yet he knew that if he worked his way out, he might be found before the ship sailed. The ship swarmed with crew members storing cargo. Men stood on the canvas and sat on it to rest. Only luck kept Billy from being crushed by a big work shoe or having some two-hundred-pound man use him as a cushion.

There was even more danger. He ran the risk of being crushed to death should a crate or box be piled on top of the canvas. Billy longed to fill his lungs with fresh, clean air, for the air under the canvas grew stale and foul.

Then he had to face the other dangers. First, his

nose itched, and when he scratched it, the itching moved to his arm, leg, and back until his whole body tingled. The itching made him furious, for if Billy moved around too much, he would surely be discovered. He wanted to turn and twist but somehow forced himself to lie still.

No sooner had the itching stopped than Billy's throat began to tickle and he had to cough. A sneezing fit followed the coughing spell. It seemed impossible that no one heard him. But Billy was lucky. Just as his coughing and sneezing fit came on, a cargo net broke and dumped its whole load of tinned goods.

The cases bounced on the deck with a terrible crash. One box broke open and cans were scattered all over. The shouting and the noise drowned out any sounds Billy might have made. By the time order was restored, he was over his sneezing and his hiding place remained safe.

The loading took several hours. Then the last steps died away and the voices faded. The *Monitor's* creaking as she bobbed and rocked at anchor was the only sound Billy could hear. He shifted his position slightly and listened to the far-off noises. The strange quiet and the darkness made him restless. He was hungry, but he did not dare to come out. The ship was still at the dock and they could put him on shore. He had to wait until the *Monitor* was at sea before leaving his hiding place.

Thirst made his lips and tongue feel dry. He closed his eyes and saw glass after glass of ice-cold water, with frozen beads on the outsides of the glasses. He remembered a drink from a fast-running brook in the cool woods; he licked his lips.

Suddenly, he was tired; fear began to gnaw at him. "I am a fool," he thought. "What am I doing here? I can't help anybody. I can't help save Tom or the ship!"

In Billy's mind, the *Monitor* was already lost. He tried to fight down the growing fear taking hold of him. All at once, the canvas covering him became a smothering blanket. He could not breathe. With a little cry of fright, Billy crawled from beneath the canvas.

Deep in the quiet dark, Billy could not know that everyone, from the engine-room crew to Captain Worden, had fears just like his own about the *Monitor*.

As soon as the iron-clad was finished, it had steamed out of the Brooklyn Navy Yard on two or three short trial voyages, but this was the first time she would sail on such a long voyage.

When the lines were hauled up and the *Monitor* had slipped from the pier, the sailors lined the flat deck and raised a mighty cheer. Workmen on the dock waved their caps and yelled a farewell. Billy knew from the noise and the hiss of the engines that the ship was under way. Little did he know he was missing the stirring farewell that the people on the shore were giving the *Monitor*.

At the end of the pier, the Navy Yard band tooted

loudly, playing such tunes as "Rally 'Round the Flag," "The Battle Hymn of the Republic," and "Columbia, the Gem of the Ocean." It was a stirring send-off, made even more so when Commodore Hiram Paulding, the Navy Yard Commander, and his staff of officers took a position on the very end of the pier to salute the *Monitor* as she passed.

At Paulding's command, the officers drew their swords, which shone in the morning sunlight as they flashed out in a farewell salute.

Word that the *Monitor* was sailing had spread among the people living near the Navy Yard. Shop-keepers closed their stores, women left their kitchens, and dozens of boys and girls came trooping to the river bank to watch the iron ship pass by.

"God bless you, lads!" an old man called out, as he waved a handkerchief at the men on the *Monitor's* deck.

A young woman wept silently, and the two young children clinging to her apron also burst into tears.

"Now, now, what's all this?" a policeman asked. "It's no time for tears."

"My husband is on the *Monitor*," the woman sobbed.

The policeman smoothed his mustache and cleared his throat. "Lady, it's nothing for you to be getting upset about. The *Monitor* will be coming back soon and she will win a great victory over that Rebel ship. She will be coming back without a scratch."

"I wish I could believe that," the woman said, drying

her tears and comforting the weeping children. "But the truth is that no one really knows if the *Monitor* can make an ocean voyage, let alone win her fight with the *Merrimack*."

She had expressed in words the thoughts of the hundreds who lined the banks of the river and looked out at the strange-looking ship moving like a clumsy duck on her way to the open sea.

John Ericsson, the man who designed the *Monitor*, was on hand at the pier to watch the vessel's leaving.

John Ericsson

He was standing with Commodore Paulding and the officers.

"Well, Mr. Ericsson, she is on her way," Paulding said. "How do you feel?"

"I am sure of success. My ship will live up to all I have hoped for her."

"Mr. Ericsson, I trust that you are right. However, as you know, I have never shared your thoughts about the merits of the *Monitor*. To me, your ship is a foolish risk and no credit to the United States Navy."

"Commodore, you will change your mind," Ericsson said. "The *Monitor* will prove herself in this battle."

"Maybe so," a young officer observed. "But it seems to me that the Rebel ship has it all over yours, Mr. Ericsson."

"We are sending those poor lads out to their deaths on that tin can there," another officer said, pointing at the *Monitor*.

Ericsson smiled. "Luckily, President Lincoln and Mr. Welles, the Secretary of the Navy, do not think as you do, gentlemen. Remember this: the day of the old Navy is ended. Your beautiful wooden sailing war-ships belong in museums. I know the *Monitor* looks strange and ugly to you. But she will yet save the nation and keep the high seas open for the United States."

With those words, Ericsson bowed politely to Commodore Paulding and the Navy officers, turned on his heel and walked away. His blue eyes twinkled behind the lenses of his silver-framed glasses. A breeze ruffled his untrimmed beard. Even though Ericsson was dressed in working clothes, he held his head high.

Commodore Paulding turned and looked after him with admiration.

"I don't know if he is right or wrong," Paulding said, "but, however things turn out, I have to admit that he is quite a man."

By this time the *Monitor* had rounded a bend in the river and disappeared from view. Only the black plume of smoke from her stack trailed after her like a long, dark feather.

She splashed out into the harbor, which was dotted with ships of all types. There were ocean-going vessels, clipper ships, packet boats, cargo ships. Some were steam-boats, some were powered by both sail and steam.

The ship masts stood out like trees bare of leaves—a huge forest, moving and swaying as though tossed by the wind.

New York harbor, the busiest port in the world, held vessels of all kinds—but nothing like the *Monitor* had ever before sailed its waters. The men on the sailing ships rushed to the rails and eyed the strange craft weaving its way between the anchored ships. A Navy cutter broke out all its signal flags in greeting to the iron-clad. The guns on Governor's Island boomed in salute, as did those of Fort Columbus and Fort LaFayette, the two big forts that guarded the harbor.

With this noisy farewell, the *Monitor* plowed on through the Narrows into the Lower Bay and out to the Atlantic Ocean on her way to Norfolk. Deep in her hold, a sixteen-year-old boy stood up in the dark, his heart pounding.

6

TROUBLE BELOW DECK

Now the men on the iron ship had their first real test in deep water. The *Monitor* bucked and tossed in the rough waves of the Atlantic. Waves washed over her low deck and the men on deck watch were drenched with sea water.

In the crew's quarters, the off-duty men lay in their hammocks and talked about the ship. The big room was hot, for it was located below the main deck.

"Man and boy, I have been in the Navy nearly twenty years and I never saw the likes of this tub," a red-bearded sailor growled, mopping his sweaty forehead with a towel.

"Aye, that is the truth," a strapping gunner said. "Here I was with good quarters on the *Hartford*, as fine a ship as ever went under sail. I am old enough to know better

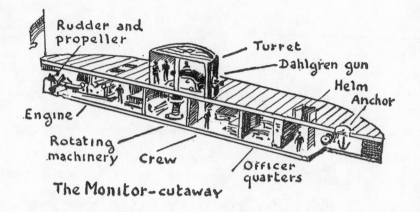

Rudder and propeller · Turret · Dahlgren gun · Helm · Anchor · Engine · Rotating machinery · Crew · Officer quarters

The Monitor-cutaway

—but I accepted duty on this tin box. Of my own free will, mind!"

"Ah, shut up, Duncan," another seaman said. "We all came aboard the same way! You aren't anything special."

Duncan glared at him. "Nobody is asking you, Matthews. Keep your nose out of my business."

Matthews sat up and swung out of his hammock, bare feet slapping on the iron floor. "Any time you want to make something out of it, just say the word! I would enjoy whipping the likes of you!"

Duncan threw up his fists. "Come on, you bag of wind! Come on!"

The two men squared away, glaring at each other. The other sailors quickly formed a circle.

"Quit your gabbing and start fighting!" a man cried.

But before a blow could be struck, Chief Petty Officer Ed Healey burst into the room. "Stop that!" he bellowed.

"You will all have fighting a-plenty, before long. Save it for the Rebs!"

"Come on, Chief," one of the sailors said. "Let them blow off steam. A good scrap will clear the air."

Healey shook a huge fist. "I am telling you to stop that talk! There will be no fighting while I am in charge here! The first man that thinks different is going to get a taste of this!" He shook his fist again.

Nobody made a move. Duncan and Matthews went back to their hammocks again. Healey put his hands on his hips and stared around the room at the men.

"A fine bunch you are! Every mother's son here is scared green, that's what is ailing the lot of you!" he snapped. "Sure, you were all big heroes when it came to accepting this special duty. But now that the fat's in the fire, you are turning yellow!"

"It is not that, Chief," Duncan protested. "We aren't afraid of the Rebels. It's this blasted crate. Look at the way she is rolling. And the sea smooth as a baby's skin."

"Sure! We don't know if she will turn turtle and drag us all down to Davy Jones's locker!" a gray-haired sailor said.

"Yeah, and here we are heading for a battle with the *Merrimack* what's carryin' ten guns while we have those two pea-shooters top side," the gunner exclaimed.

Healey stood stock-still and looked hard at the men. "There isn't a man jack among you that's fit to call himself a member of Uncle Sam's Navy! You aren't using

63

the brains the good Lord gave you! Think for a minute. Our skipper is the bravest, best sailor in the fleet. There's Lieutenant Tom Hurst—a better man never walked a quarter-deck—and the pea-shooters, as you call them, are Dahlgren guns, the finest cannon made, guns that can blast anything out of the water!"

"But they are only two against the Rebs' ten," the gunner answered.

"The Rebs can have fifty guns! One Dahlgren can shoot faster, farther and hit harder than any piece that was ever made," Healey roared.

A look of shame came over the gunner's face. "You know, Chief, maybe you are right. Maybe we are all suffering from a bad case of cold feet!"

"There's no maybe about it!" Healey shouted. "You are acting like a bunch of greenhorns. You, Duncan, you have smelled gun powder before. And Matthews, you have sailed on tubs that leaked so badly they had to keep the pumps going the minute they lifted anchor. I know what's eating all of you. This ship is something new—and that is what scares you!"

"Hey, Chief, you think we have stage fright, huh?" Duncan smiled.

"I know it! Now stop acting like a pack of dry-land sailors. The *Monitor* isn't going to turn over. We will lick the *Merrimack* and we ought to be darn proud to be aboard the first iron ship in the Union Navy," Healey said.

Duncan threw up his hands. "Okay, I give up. You have talked sense into me."

"That's the kind of talk," Healey said. "I would have done it one way or the other. By talking or"—he held up his fist—"by pounding. Now, let's have an end to this gab. Let me tell you something—old Abe Lincoln himself put his okay on the *Monitor*. And what's good enough for Mr. Lincoln is good enough for me! Now put that in your pipe and smoke it!" Healey hitched his gun belt tighter. "I am going up on deck to make my rounds. When I come back, I want to see a crew of happy sailors —or I will beat the tar out of the lot of you!"

Without another word, Healey swung around and left the room, slamming the big iron door shut behind him.

"You know," Duncan said, "he can do just that, too."

"Aye," the gunner nodded. "I am more scared of Ed Healey than of this ship or the Rebs. Let's settle down now, lads. We are all in the same boat, so there is no use stewing about it."

The *Monitor* splashed on toward Norfolk. Her crew still tasted the fear that comes of not knowing what is going to happen—but now they controlled it.

Courage, the sailors had learned from Healey, was built on faith. They had to believe in Captain Worden, in the *Monitor* itself, and in the Stars and Stripes that fluttered from her flag mast.

They were in a war fighting for a cause which they felt was a just one. Now the time had come to show they had the courage to fight and, if need be, to die for that cause.

Billy, below decks, peered out into the gloom.

A ship's lantern, turned low, cast a tiny spot of light over in one corner. Now that he was in the open, some of Billy's fears began to fade away. He felt more cheerful in spite of the hunger and thirst. He could do nothing about it just now—food and drink would come later.

He did not care if it was only bread and water, when they found out that he had sneaked aboard. "Anyway, if the *Monitor* is going to be sunk, I will be with Tom," he thought.

He waited a long time until the pitch of the ship told him she was in deep water. "Well," he murmured, "I may as well go up and face the music. I hope they aren't too rough on me."

He groped his way slowly toward the light. The cargo was stacked in proper fashion. Provisions were stored together on one side. Tools, spare parts and other supplies were lashed in place on the other.

Now that she was at sea, the *Monitor* dipped and pitched sharply. Billy had to hang on to keep on his feet. He had never been on a ship at sea before and silently prayed that he would not get seasick.

So far, he had seen no one. It was as though he were the only passenger on a ghost ship. If anyone had been around, it would have been easy enough to spot Billy.

No matter how carefully he walked, a sudden movement of the ship sent him flying against a crate or a case. He cried out when he hit; the sharp edges hurt. Once he knocked over a big metal drum. It fell with such a crash that Billy was sure it had been heard from one end of the ship to the other. He froze in terror and waited for flashing lanterns and angry voices as the sailors closed in on him. Nothing happened and nobody came after him.

He went on looking for a ship's ladder that led to the upper deck. Finally, he found one that led below where bags of sand were stored to keep the ship riding level. Another ran to the upper deck. A lighted ship's lantern hung at the foot of this ladder.

Billy was just ready to go up when he heard steps and voices. Ducking back into the shadows, he pressed flat against the wall.

Two sailors came along, each carrying a heavy bag balanced on a shoulder. They paused at the bottom of the stairs, where one of the men lowered the bag he held and turned to his companion.

"I think you are crazy, Jed. We can't get away with this."

"Why don't you shut up, Wes?" the other man snapped, as he, too, set down his bag.

"But, Jed, listen."

"I said shut up! I know what I am doing, Wes!"

"Sure. But what if we meet an officer and he starts asking questions; what then?"

67

Gretna School Library

"You worry too much. Don't you know the Navy by
now? Look as though you are working and nobody will
bother you—not even old Abe Lincoln."

"I am not worried about Lincoln. It is the officers on
this ship. If one of them wonders why we are carrying
bags of sand about, what are we supposed to say?"

The man called Jed frowned at Wes. "Orders! Orders!
We were told to shift the bags by the Captain."

Wes shook his head in doubt. "Well, maybe, but I sure
wish we had a better story."

"And I wish I had a partner with some nerve," Jed said
with scorn.

"You think I am yellow?" Wes said.

"I didn't say that. You worry too much. Now, hear this. Anybody asks what we are doing, this is a work order. We were told to move these bags below, up forward— do you get it?"

"Yes," Wes nodded.

Billy stood there, listening and wondering about the men. He had never seen these two sailors before—but then, not even he knew all the men in the *Monitor's* crew. Besides, the men were probably only trying to dodge some backbreaking job by this trick.

"Okay, if you understand, Wes, then let's stop talking about it and haul anchor." Jed swung the bag over his shoulder again. As he did, his right hand rested in the glow of the lantern for an instant. Billy smothered a cry. In the circle of light, he saw, or thought he had seen, a rearing horse tattooed on the back of Jed's right hand. The very same mark that he saw on the man who tried to burn the *Monitor*. But the next second, Jed started to climb the stairs. Wes reached out and stopped him.

"What's the matter?" Jed asked, annoyed.

"Listen, I heard something. It sounded like someone in the dark there." He pointed at the exact spot where Billy was hiding.

Jed shook his head. "You do have it bad, don't you, Wes? Why, you are more nervous than my old Aunt Matilda. Come on."

"I heard something, I tell you," Wes repeated.

"Sure you did. The waves slapping against this tub."

69

"I guess I am a little nervous," Wes said.

"A little?" Jed laughed. "You are like a dog with a tin can tied to his tail. Now let's go, before I get mad."

"Don't be so smart," Wes muttered. He picked up his bag and the two men went up the ladder to the deck.

Beads of cold sweat popped out on Billy's forehead. He leaned back against the wall, grateful for the cold feeling of the metal. "Phew! At least they didn't come looking for me. That was too close," he thought.

He wondered about Jed. Had he really seen the horse tattoo on the sailor's hand or had it been just a trick of his imagination?

Billy frowned. Why should the man he was looking for run the risk of being seen again here on the *Monitor*? "I would know him in a minute," Billy thought. "Just one look at him and I would know." He paused and his frown grew deeper. For all at once he realized that he could not say for sure who the man with the tattoo was.

"I have never seen his face—not really. He was masked the first time we met, and just now he was in the shadow most of the time. I couldn't pick him or his friend out of a group. If he is the man we are after, he is still pretty safe," Billy thought.

If only he could be sure about the tattoo. "I could go right to the Captain and tell him. But I have no proof. He won't believe me. More than likely he would think I was trying to cover up for sneaking aboard like this," Billy said to himself. "What a mess!"

He paused at the foot of the ladder. The thing for him to do was find Tom. He would know how to handle this problem. Billy went up the steps. Once on deck, he knew how to get around the ship. But he had to be careful. If he were caught before he got to Tom, he would have a hard time making anyone believe his story.

He first went to Tom's cabin, but his friend was not there. Tom was either on watch or in the officers' room. Billy decided to try that room first.

In order to reach it, he had to pass by the ship's kitchen, called the galley, where the cook was hard at work cleaning up after serving early meals to the men. Billy's mouth watered as he smelled stew and coffee. For a moment, he struggled against a desire to enter and beg the cook for something to eat. He closed his eyes as he fought down his hunger.

He forced himself to go on to the officers' room. Talk and laughter drifted to him through the swinging doors which flapped back and forth with the ship's motion. Billy sneaked up to the doors and peeked inside.

Several of the *Monitor's* officers were there, seated in chairs, smoking and talking. He saw Tom Hurst, puffing on his pipe, talking to Captain Worden. Billy tried to get Tom's attention from the doorway by signaling with his hands.

He was so busy seeking to catch Tom's eye that he did not notice a sailor coming up behind him. The sailor very quietly snapped the button on his gun case

71

and drew a revolver. He pushed the gun into the small of Billy's back.

"All right, now," he said in a sharp voice. "Make a move and I shoot. Understand?"

"Yes," Billy said, and tried to keep his knees from knocking together.

7

THE CAPTAIN'S DECISION

The revolver poked into Billy's back for what seemed to him a very long time. Actually, less than a minute passed before the voice said, "All right. Turn around, real slow. Let's get a look at you!"

Billy obeyed and came face to face with Officer Ed Healey, who looked at him in wonder.

"Billy! Aren't you a long way from your shoe-shine stand?" Healey said.

"That's so," Billy admitted. He mopped his forehead with a handkerchief. "Golly, Chief, you scared me half to death! My knees are still doing a jig!"

Healey laughed. "Sorry, Billy. It is my watch and I saw you sneaking around. Of course, I caught you."

"Of course," Billy said. "Say, will you do me a favor?"

"What is it?"

"Put away that gun, Chief. I wouldn't want it to go off by accident."

Healey slipped the big revolver back into its case, or holster. "That make you feel better?"

Billy nodded.

"Now, would you mind telling me what you are doing aboard this ship?"

"Well, Chief," Billy began, "I decided to go along on the trip, so I hid in some canvas."

Healey put his hands on his hips and frowned at Billy. "Ah, you did, did you? And what was all that hand-waving and signaling a few minutes ago?"

"Oh, I wanted to get Tom's—I mean Lieutenant Hurst's—attention. I wanted him to know I was on board."

Healey's hand shot out to grab Billy by the collar. "Wanted his attention, eh? Then you will have it! And Captain Worden's, too! We don't take kindly to boys hiding on Uncle Sam's ships."

Billy moved around in the grip that held him like a steel trap. "Wait, Chief! You know me! Why are you treating me like this?"

"Orders, lad, orders," Healey said. "Now, to the officers' room! March!" He shoved Billy through the swinging doors.

All the officers stared in surprise as they entered.

"Billy!" Tom exclaimed.

"What is this, Healey?" Captain Worden asked.

"I found him outside this door," Healey said, still holding tightly to Billy's collar.

"What!" Tom gulped.

"Now, now, calm down, Lieutenant Hurst," Captain Worden said. "Release the prisoner, Healey."

The officer let Billy go. Captain Worden called to him. "Come here, lad."

Billy stepped forward. His heart was beating so hard that it drummed in his ears.

"What is your story? How did you get aboard my ship without being seen?" the Captain asked.

"I . . . I hid in a roll of canvas and was hauled aboard," Billy said in a trembling voice.

A smile flickered on the Captain's lips. "Came aboard with the cargo, eh? That is an old trick. Why did you do it?"

"Well, sir, I . . . I . . ."

"Go ahead, son."

Billy drew himself up straight. "I wanted to fight the Rebels, sir!"

Captain Worden nodded seriously. "I see. And do you think the United States Navy needs boys as young as you to fight its battles?"

"I am sixteen years old, sir! There are drummer boys in the Army younger than I!" Billy said.

"That is true. But this is the Navy. However, I like your spirit, lad. I was not much older than you when I first went to sea." The Captain cleared his throat. "But that is neither here nor there. Do you know how the Navy treats boys who hide on ships?"

"No, sir," Billy gulped.

"Puts them in irons in the brig—the ship's prison—and feeds them bread and water!" Captain Worden growled fiercely. "What do you think of that?"

"Not much," Billy said. He was getting more and more

scared. To be locked in a dark room with chains on his hands and feet and nothing to eat except bread and water did not seem a very pleasant thing.

Captain Worden turned from Billy and winked at Tom. "Lieutenant Hurst, I believe you know this young man!"

"Aye, sir!" Tom said slowly.

"Do you think he wants to fight the Rebels?"

Tom thought for a moment. "Perhaps, sir. I am willing to go along with his statement."

"Tom!" Billy cried. "You are not being fair! I have told you a hundred times that I want to go off and fight for the Union! Well, this time I decided to do something about it!"

"Just a moment!" Captain Worden snapped. "I have a word to say. The fact remains that you are on this ship without any right to be here. Now, what am I to do about that?"

"I don't know, sir," Billy said, lowering his eyes.

"I shall tell you then, my lad. A court of officers will meet and decide your punishment. Now, I have a question to ask you," Captain Worden said in a stern voice.

"Yes, sir?"

"When did you eat last?"

"I had breakfast early this morning, sir," Billy replied, puzzled by the Captain's question.

"It would not be right for the Navy to order a hungry boy put on a diet of bread and water," Captain Worden

78

smiled. "Lieutenant Hurst, take the prisoner to the galley and tell cook to feed him. Then bring him back here."

"Aye, sir," Tom said. "Come along, Billy."

As they left the room, there was a burst of laughter from the officers. Billy glanced at Tom in surprise.

"What is so funny?" he asked.

"Beats me," Tom said. "Maybe putting you in irons seems funny to them."

"Well, I don't see anything to laugh about," Billy said.

"You should have thought of that before you sneaked aboard," Tom scolded.

Billy eyed his friend. "You are angry with me, aren't you?" he asked.

"You would hardly expect this fool stunt to please me, would you?" Tom's voice was sharp. "After all, I am in a fix, too. Everyone knows we are friends."

"Tom, I am sorry," Billy said. His face showed his gloom.

"Sorry! I bet you are sorry. Why, I ought to tan your hide, but I won't," Tom grinned. "You must not have been very comfortable hiding in that folded canvas."

"That's for sure. I thought I would smother." Billy paused for a moment. "Are you still mad?"

Tom ruffled Billy's hair. "Oh, just a bit annoyed, but I will get over that."

Billy felt as though a weight had been lifted from him. He could not bear the thought of losing Tom Hurst's friendship.

"Taking a shot at the Rebels wasn't your only reason for hiding on the ship, was it?" Tom asked.

Billy shook his head. "I saw a chance to go with you and I grabbed it."

Tom grinned. "I figure we make a team, lad. It is lonely without a family. I know." He sighed. "Well, enough of this talk. It took a lot of courage to sneak on to the *Monitor*. I am glad to have you aboard. Very glad."

"Thanks, Tom." Billy smiled. "But I am not out of trouble yet. What will Captain Worden do to me?"

"That is hard to say. I have seen him toss men into the brig for a lot less. Gave them the full punishment, too. Irons and a bread-and-water diet. Right up to the limit of the law. One full week."

"A week? I would never make it," Billy swallowed hard.

"Oh, he has done even worse. Sometimes, he would have a man whipped for good measure. Why, he has the right to tie you to the mast and give you ten lashes! That is according to naval rules."

"Golly!" Billy whispered, gulping hard.

"However, since this ship does not have the right kind of mast and I haven't seen a whip on board, I would say you were not in much danger," Tom laughed. "Now let's find out what cook can scrape up for you."

A bit later, Billy was perched on a high stool. Mike Durgan, the cook, set down before him a plate heaped with stew and potatoes. A tin platter filled with hot biscuits and a large mug of coffee completed the meal.

"Dig in there, boy!" the cook cried. "You can search the seven seas over and you will not be finding stew and biscuits to equal these. Ask any sailor in the U. S. Navy who dishes out the best food, and they will tell you it is Mike Durgan!"

"If your cooking matched your bragging, Mike, you would be the finest cook in the whole world, let alone the U. S. Navy," Tom said.

Mike Durgan puffed out his chest, curled the ends of his mustache and nodded in agreement. "That is the truth, Lieutenant. The real truth!"

"Mike, you are the best, and that is no fooling," Tom laughed.

"Thank you, sir, Mike Durgan thanks you for your praise," the cook said.

Billy ate fast, gulping the food, and in a short time he had wiped the plate clean with a scrap of the last biscuit.

Tom and Mike watched as the boy satisfied his hunger. "No matter what Captain Worden decides about you, Billy, you are going to be punished on a full stomach," Tom laughed.

"Mmm . . . that's so," Billy said, licking his lips. "What food! Mike, you are the greatest cook alive. Why, you should be head cook of the entire Navy."

"Thanks, boy," Mike said. He swept off his tall cook's hat and bowed low. As he did so, Billy noticed for the first time a tattoo mark on the back of the cook's right hand.

He jumped up, tingling with excitement. "Tom! Look at that tattoo on Mike's hand!"

"What about it?" Tom said. "It is only a black horse galloping like the wind."

Mike held up his huge hand. "Sure, there isn't anything special . . ."

"Yes, there is," Billy cried. "The horse!"

"The horse?" Tom asked.

"It is the same horse that was tattooed on the man who tried to burn the ship. And I saw that man on this ship when I came out of my hiding place a few minutes ago."

"Billy, are you sure?" Tom gripped the boy's arm. "Are you sure?"

Billy told Tom then about the two sailors who had been carrying the bags of sand and how he thought he had seen the rearing-horse tattoo on the hand of one of the men.

Tom listened with a look of surprise. "There was no order given to move sand. I made out the duty list myself." He stared hard at Billy. "You didn't dream up this yarn, did you?"

"You know better than that, Tom. I saw those two men and the tattoo mark."

"Some new men came aboard this morning," Tom said. "There was no chance to talk with them. Aside from them, I would stand up for every man in this crew," Tom said.

"Lieutenant," the cook cut in, "I was just thinking about this tattoo of mine. I got it when I served on the old *Biscayne Bay*. You were just new then, doing your first duty as an officer. Remember?"

"Of course I do. But what has that to do with your tattoo?" Tom asked.

"We were down in Charleston back in '58," Mike said. "I went on liberty with three men out of Number 9 gun crew and we found this tattoo artist. He did a job on each of us. The same horse—standing, running, jumping, rearing."

"Mike! Who were the men?" Tom asked eagerly.

"I would like to help, Lieutenant, but it has been a long time. I can't remember too well. Charlie Hegan was there, Tim Spencer and another one. He didn't stay with the *Biscayne Bay* very long." Mike shook his head. "Sorry, his name slips me now."

"Any of those men might be the one we are after," Tom said.

"Hegan and Spencer are on the *Kearsage* in the Atlantic Squadron, so that lets them out," Mike said. "If I can only think of that other fellow's name . . ."

"Meanwhile, the man we want may be loose on this ship." Tom pounded his fist into the palm of his left hand. "Billy, we have to get back to Captain Worden."

"Sure, Tom. Thanks again, Mike," Billy said.

They walked in silence for a few seconds. At last, Billy said, "Tom, we must find that tattooed man!"

83

"I wish Mike could remember his name." Tom frowned. "I was on the *Biscayne Bay* for almost a year as an officer of the gun crew. I should be able to remember the gun crews. Let's see Number 9 gun . . ."

But before Tom could go any further a bell began to clang. A bugle sounded. "General quarters! Go to general quarters!" a voice bawled loudly.

"What is going on?" Billy asked.

"I don't know, but something is wrong! That was the gun-tower alarm bell. Stay close behind me, Billy!" Tom shouted as he ran down the passage.

8

THE MISSING MEN

There was a delay of only seconds before the *Monitor's* crew sprang to obey the alarm. Even as Billy raced along the passage, he heard shouting, "Look alive, you men! Man your battle stations! Move!"

Officers came running from their room buckling on sword belts. The alarm bell pealed again, and its sound was like a cry for help.

Sailors came piling out of the crew's quarters. Some men were armed with pistols and knives. Others carried rifles. Some men dragged boxes of shells. An elevator, worked by hand, hauled heavy shells up to the gun tower from below deck.

Billy came to the gun tower a few steps behind Tom, who pulled open the iron door.

A gray-eyed sailor, a long-time Navy man, saluted Tom. "What in blazes is happening up here, Wilkins?" the Lieutenant demanded. "Who rang the alarm bell?"

"Sir—I did!" Wilkins said.

Tom glanced around the tower. Billy followed his gaze. The boy had never before been in the tower, which sat in the middle of the ship like a huge iron barrel. The guns poked out of firing slits through which the crew chief aimed his gun by raising or lowering the wheels on the cannon.

A cone-shaped iron roof covered the tower and protected the men inside from enemy shells. A clocklike machine worked by a series of cranks and levers gave the power for turning the tower.

There was a tube through which the officer in the

tower could speak to the wheel house, the engine room and the Captain's quarters.

"You sounded the alarm and ordered general quarters, Wilkins?" Tom asked.

"Aye, sir," the Gunner's Mate replied.

"Did you sight an enemy ship?"

"No, sir."

"Then speak up, man! Why in the name of reason did you do it?"

"Sir, I will be in the Navy twenty-three years come September. Man and boy, I have sailed with the fleet. But never have I run up against anything like this!" Wilkins said.

"Wilkins! What are you talking about?" Tom roared.

"We are on a bad-luck ship, sure enough." The Mate sighed and looked around at the tight-lipped gun crews. "These lads will bear me out, sir. It is none of my doing. I keep this tower clean as a whistle. There isn't a speck of dust that I allow—"

"Have you gone crazy, man?" Tom said. "You are not making sense, Wilkins."

"Sand, sir! Sand in the guns. Sand in the tower revolving gears. Bags and bags of sand dumped into my tower—now the guns don't work and the tower can't revolve. The *Monitor* is helpless!" Wilkins moaned.

"What?" Tom cried. "Is this right, men?" he asked the gun crews.

"Aye, sir," a gunner nodded sadly. "Aye."

At that moment, the tower door was flung open and Captain Worden burst in. He was followed by a half dozen staff officers.

"Attention!" Tom bawled.

"Who ordered general quarters?" Captain Worden shouted. "I will skin him alive!"

The Captain was pale with anger, and Billy drew back into a corner, to make himself as small as possible.

"I am the man, sir," Wilkins said. "I think I did the right thing when I discovered things up here."

"You *think!*" Captain Worden bellowed. "What did you discover?"

"The tower revolving gears and the two guns have been fouled with sand," Wilkins said. "I brought the gun crews in for extra drill and discovered this sand. I thought, sir, that I had best alert the vessel without reporting it to any higher ranking officer."

Captain Worden cleared his throat. "I see. You were right, Wilkins." He glanced at the officers grouped behind him. "Gentlemen, check the damage and let me know how soon repairs can be made!"

Headed by Wilkins, the officers started inspecting the gears and the guns. Captain Worden called to Tom. "Hurst, what do you make of this?" he asked.

Tom shook his head. "It must have been done with intent, sir."

"Yes. If Wilkins had not called the special gun drill, we might not have found out until tomorrow that the guns and tower were not working," Captain Worden said. "And that would have been too late. I expect to be fighting the *Merrimack* within another day."

"That suits me fine, sir," Tom said.

"You won't be so eager if this mess is not straightened out," Worden said, pointing at the tower. "How is it coming, gentlemen?" he asked the officers who were peering into the guns and examining the tower gears.

"We can put everything in order, sir," the damage-control officer reported. "I believe it will take about twenty-four hours."

"Twenty-four hours! Listen, mister, you will do it in eight!" Captain Worden roared.

"But, sir—" the officer protested.

"But me no buts!" Worden shouted. "Take all the men you need—but get this job done! Now, snap to it!"

"Aye, sir," said the officer.

"Anybody here who can help me find out who tried to wreck my ship better speak up," Worden said, as he swung to face the crew.

Billy stepped forward slowly. "I think I can help, sir."

The captain's eyes flashed at the boy. "Then say your piece, lad! Don't stand there shaking in your boots."

Billy told the captain what he had seen and heard while hiding in the ship. As he talked, the tower hummed with activity. Hastily grouped work parties reported for duty. The gun crews started the long job of cleaning out the barrels of the cannon. Others began work on the gears.

When Billy finished, Tom added the details about the tattoo artist and the four men from the *Biscayne Bay.*

"I want to see the men who reported aboard yesterday, Lieutenant. Also, have section leaders check their groups. The tattooed man is aboard. Find him!" Captain Worden ordered.

"Aye, sir!" Tom said. "I will send word to section leaders at once."

"Very good. Bring the new men to the officers' room," Worden snapped. He pointed a finger at Billy. "Come with me, lad."

Billy walked with Captain Worden to the officers' room and, when they were inside, waited for the Captain to speak. Worden took an old pipe from his pocket and filled it with tobacco. He struck a match, puffed for a while and then cocked his head at Billy.

"Nothing like a good smoke to calm a man's nerves. But I reckon you are a bit young for tobacco."

"I don't smoke, sir," Billy said in a polite voice, at the same time quite nervous about the Captain's reasons for asking him here.

"You are a sensible lad, Billy," the Captain said. "I have not made up my mind what to do with you. I could make things pretty hot, you know that, don't you?"

"Yes, sir," Billy said. He could feel the cold sweat breaking out on his forehead.

"Aye, I could make it hot—and not too comfortable," Worden said, pointing his pipe at Billy. "But I have now decided to give you a chance." He paused, drew a few puffs on the pipe and then blew out a cloud of smoke. "Just before general quarters was sounded, I talked it over with my board of officers."

Billy found it hard to swallow. Now the palms of his hands were sweating and his heart pounded. He could not remember when he had been more frightened and nervous than he was at this moment.

"Aye, I talked it over with the court and we reached a decision. Are you prepared to hear it?"

"Yes, sir," Billy said in a small voice, bracing himself for whatever was coming.

Just then, Tom Hurst rushed into the room. He was alone and his face showed his worry.

"Where are those men, Lieutenant?" Worden asked.

Tom shook his head. "I don't know, sir. They both had been given duty in the engine room, but neither was at his station."

"Nonsense! They must be somewhere on the ship. Men cannot disappear in the middle of the ocean!"

"It seems these two men can. I checked through the roll and found them listed under the names of Seth Turner and Kenneth Tuthill. It happens that Turner and Tuthill are men with whom I served on the *Quincy* several years ago." Tom doubled his fists to hold back his rising anger. "Both of them were wounded during the attack on Fort Hatteras last August when the *Quincy* was sunk—and were still in the hospital last week."

"But the men who reported had papers," Captain Worden said. "Who checked them?"

"The duty officer—Lieutenant Marcy. But it was not his fault. They had proper papers. Stolen from Turner and Tuthill at the hospital."

"Of course," Captain Worden agreed. "That has happened before. A Rebel agent in the hospital could easily have done it." He puffed so hard on his pipe that his head was surrounded by a cloud of blue tobacco smoke. "We have to find those two men, Lieutenant. Get a search party and hunt them out."

"I will search the ship for them, sir," Tom said. He saluted and left the room.

"Those Rebels!" he growled. "I will string them up when we find them!"

Billy approached him and said, "Sir, what about me?"

The Captain frowned as though seeing him for the first time. "You? Oh, yes, yes. We need a cabin boy for this trip. Is that all right with you?"

"I am not to be punished?" Billy cried happily.

"Oh, you are not getting off lightly, lad. There will be plenty of work for you. And danger, too. Fighting the *Merrimack* will not be a picnic," Captain Worden said.

"Captain, I . . . I . . . thank you, sir. You will find that I am a good hard worker." Billy shook his head. "Golly, things couldn't be better."

"I am glad you think so, son, but I won't be content until your tattooed friend and his partner are safely in irons," the Captain said, as he laid his pipe aside.

"Yes, sir," Billy said. He wished with all his heart that he might find the men. It would be a way to show his gratitude. He saw himself with all the officers shaking his hand and the Captain pinning a medal on him. It was a grand dream, soon broken when Captain Worden said, "Harper, fetch me a cup of coffee, and stop dreaming!"

"Right away, Captain!" Billy said, blushing.

He rushed out. A group of sailors, led by Tom, filed toward him.

"Any luck?" he asked.

"Not a trace," Tom said, signaling the men to halt. "How did you make out?"

"Very well," Billy smiled. "Very well. I am to be cabin boy on this trip."

Tom clapped him on the shoulder. "See that you do a good job." He turned to the sailors. "Let's go, lads. We will search the stern of the ship while it is still daylight."

Billy stepped to one side as the sailors went past. He heard their steps sounding on the metal deck long after they had turned the corner.

He rushed on to the kitchen. "Hey, Mike," he called, when he did not see the cook, "where are you?"

There was no answer, and Billy stepped inside. "That's funny," he thought. "Mike is supposed to be on duty. He must have stepped out for a minute. Well, I don't need him to pour a cup of coffee."

A large pot bubbled on the stove. Billy found a cup

and saucer and was reaching for the coffeepot when an arm came around his throat with such strength that he gulped for air. The cup and saucer fell from his hand, to shatter on the floor.

Billy struggled, but the pressing on his throat did not ease. A red mist swam before his eyes—red, then a choking black and then nothing.

9

THE FUSE IS LIT

Billy's first thought when he opened his eyes was that he had not brought the coffee to Captain Worden. "He will think I am a pretty sorry excuse for a cabin boy," Billy told himself.

Then he felt the throbbing pain in his throat. It hurt when he swallowed and his throat felt raw and bruised. He tried to reach up and touch it, but he could not move his arms. They seemed stiff and heavy. He forced his eyes open again and blinked in surprise at what he saw.

He was in a place where sides of beef, on hooks, hung from the walls. Tubs of butter were piled up; great slabs of cheese, twenty-gallon milk cans, vegetables in crates and other foods were being stored there.

Billy saw all this by the light of a lamp that stood on

a barrel. It dawned on him suddenly that he was in the *Monitor's* huge ice box. At the same time, he realized that his hands and feet were bound. The rope bit into his wrists and ankles. His hands, tied behind his back, were so strongly lashed that he was scarcely able to move the fingers.

By stretching his neck, he could see the large slabs of ice stacked against the rear wall. It was cold, so cold that Billy saw the mist of his own breath. He turned his head from side to side and found that he was lying on the floor.

He made out the figure of Mike Durgan, propped in a sitting position. Mike was bound and gagged. The cook's head was bloody, but he was straining and pulling against the ropes, his muscles swelling with the effort.

"Mike!" Billy whispered. "Mike!"

The cook swung his head. His eyes grew wide with surprise as he saw Billy and he grunted.

"Who did this, Mike? Did you see them?" Billy asked.

Mike made some sounds and shook his head. He struggled with the rope again but saw that his efforts were of no use.

"We are in a fix, all right," Billy said.

Mike answered by nodding quickly.

Suddenly, the ice box door opened and two men entered, closing the door behind them. They were both in uniform. For a moment Billy had a touch of hope.

"What luck!" he cried. "You found us!"

"Sure, boy. You are real lucky," one of the men said.

At the sound of his voice, a chill ran through Billy. The sailor bent over him. "You know me, eh, kid?" he laughed. "Kind of know my voice, huh?"

"I have heard it before," Billy said.

"So you got out of the river," the sailor said. "I should have made sure, when I threw you into the drink." He turned to his companion. "Hey, Wes. This is the kid I was telling you about. The shoe-shine boy who wanted to be a hero!"

97

Gretna School Library

"Jed, there is no time for this. Let's finish what we have to do and pull out," Wes said.

"Keep your shirt on. I have a few things to tell my friend here." He looked at Billy again and the light from the lamp fell on his face.

Billy stared hard at the heavy brows, which hooded deep-set eyes; he had a big jaw, square chin, stern mouth and wide nose. It was a strong but cruel face. When the man smiled, he looked evil rather than pleasant.

"Think you will know me the next time you see my mug?" the man asked.

"I will never forget you!" Billy said.

"Well, take a good look—because you aren't ever going to see me again. In fact, you won't see anything when I am finished with you. You will be very nicely dead."

"Jed, for Pete's sake, stop the talking and get to work," Wes cried.

Jed waved his hands in an effort to quiet his pal and Billy saw the rearing-horse tattoo mark clearly. He shifted his gaze to Mike, who was glaring at the man, making sounds behind his gag.

The tattooed man got up and stood over Mike. "Remember me, Durgan? Ah, those were the good days aboard the *Biscayne Bay*. Will you ever forget the night we went to that tattooing parlor in Charleston?" Jed gave a nasty laugh.

Mike moved to break loose. But Jed only laughed harder. "I tied those knots. And you will recall that I was the best hand with a good rope on the old tub."

Mike growled so fiercely that he seemed about to explode. Jed cuffed him with the back of his hand. "Shut up! Another peep out of you and I will really get rough."

The cook kept quiet, but his eyes stared with hate. "That's better," Jed said. "Use what little sense you have."

Wes, who was growing more nervous by the minute, watched his friend. "Will you leave him alone and do our job?" he begged. "They may find us any time."

"All right, Wes. But we have been giving them the slip up to now. You don't think they got any smarter, do you? That clown, Tom Hurst, is leading the search party. I knew him on the *Biscayne Bay*. He was a nobody then —and he still is," Jed stated with anger.

"You think everyone is a nobody," Wes said.

Jed's deep eyes clouded in hatred. He walked back and forth and his voice rose as he talked. "They made him an officer! The likes of him, can you beat it? Here I was thrown out of the Navy in disgrace and a someone like Tom Hurst is wearing officer's stripes!" His walking became more excited. He waved his arms. "They threw me out of the Navy! I said then I would have revenge."

"Jed, keep your voice down!" Wes pleaded.

"Let them hear!"

"Don't go off like this. Remember why we are here," Wes said. "There is more to this job than helping you get even with the U. S. Navy."

99

"I know, I know," Jed muttered, passing a hand before his eyes as though brushing away cobwebs.

"If they had not found out that the tower guns and gears were fouled, we could have been off this ship long ago," Wes sighed.

"But they found out! So we will just go ahead with our other plan. How do you think I felt when the fires I set aboard the ship didn't work?" Jed shook his fist at Billy. "And that boy almost had me caught, in the bargain."

"All right, Jed, just take it easy. I am getting the powder," Wes said.

He went to the back of the ice box and felt around among some cases and crates. A moment later, he said, "I have it, Jed."

"Okay, Wes. I told you it would be there." Jed rubbed his hands together and smiled at Mike and Billy. "Hey, cook! We have been keeping a little surprise right here in your ice box," he said.

Wes returned, carrying a small barrel which he set down near Jed. "The fuse and matches are under the lid," he said.

"Get the butcher knife hanging over the cook's work table and be careful nobody sees you," Jed commanded.

Wes threw him a mean look but stepped out of the ice box and came back in a few seconds. He held the large knife in his hand.

Jed reached for the tool. "Let's have it," he said.

"A man could chop down a good-sized tree with this."
He brought it down on the barrel head, which split
under the blow. "There you are, Wes."

Reaching down into the barrel, Wes found a package
wrapped in oiled paper. He opened it and took out a
long length of fuse cord and a box of matches.

Jed stepped over to Billy. "In case you are wondering
what we have in mind, I will be glad to tell you, so you
will know what is coming." He pointed to the barrel.
"That is gun powder. And that cord is a fuse. A real
slow-burning fuse. I think you can guess what is going
to happen next."

"Mister, you must be crazy!" Billy said. "You are
going to blow up the *Monitor!*"

"That's the idea, lad."

"But you will go with her!" Billy cried.

Jed rocked with laughter. "You hear that, Wes? This
boy is quite a joker."

Wes was busy with the fuse. "Forget about him, will
you? I need some help to lay out this cord."

"Sure, mate. In a minute. I want to set this lad
straight first. And I want the cook to hear it, too, because we were old shipmates." Jed leaned toward the
two prisoners. In a low tone, he said, "There is a small
life boat we have hidden near the *Monitor's* bow. Well,
after Wes and I do what has to be done, we will skip up
there, lower the boat and shove off. There is a ship
waiting to pick us up not too far away."

"You *are* crazy!" Billy exclaimed. "They will shoot you down before you reach the life boat!"

"No, they won't, lad. They will not be able to see us with night falling."

"Are you never going to quit talking and get to work?" Wes said.

Jed smiled his evil smile. "You see, we have thought of everything. Yes, sir, once this fuse is lit, we hit the

deck, take the boat and thirty minutes later, the *Monitor* won't be fit for the scrap heap."

The two men played out the fuse, put one end of it in the barrel and moved to the ice box door.

Jed struck a match, and when it came to life, he touched the lighted end to the fuse. A spark began to creep along the cord, inching toward the barrel of gun powder.

"So long, mates!" Jed boomed. "You won't feel a thing when that powder goes off. You will probably be half-frozen to death by then. It gets mighty cold in this ice box. We ought to know. This is where we hid while they were searching for us."

Wes opened the door and the men slipped out, slamming it shut behind them. Billy and Mike stared in horror at the tiny spark creeping across the ship's deck.

"Thirty minutes," Billy muttered. "I have to do something." It was useless to call for help, he knew. And Mike was tied up so tightly he could not speak or move. The thick door of the ice box would smother any shout, even if Mike should free his mouth to call out. Billy lay quietly, watching the slow progress of the spark. The temperature in the ice box was affecting him. His hands and feet were cold, his face felt stiff and frozen.

There did not seem to be a thing to do. Yet he could not simply lie there waiting for the spark to explode the powder and destroy the *Monitor*, with all aboard.

With a great desperate burst of effort, Billy began

Gretna School Library

inching toward the burning fuse. His progress was both slow and full of pain, for every movement caused the ropes to rub against his wrists and ankles.

He struggled on, like a giant crab, a few inches at a time. It looked to Billy as though he was as far from the fuse as ever. But the burning end of the fuse was much closer to the barrel of gun powder. With a final effort, Billy slid and rolled to where the fuse sparked and smoked. At last, his body was on the cord and he was smothering the spark with his body. From the other side of the ice box, Mike Durgan made a happy noise and thumped his heels on the floor.

But only half their problem was solved. Now the powder would not explode but they were still here in the ice box. They had to get out before the deadly cold killed both of them.

Billy glanced around the big ice box. Near the door, he noticed a five-gallon jug with the word "Vinegar" printed across it standing on top of a keg. He remembered from a day in Mrs. Dobbins' kitchen what it was. This looked like water and was used in cooking. It had the sharpest smell he could remember. Billy also observed a tiny light coming in under the ice box door from the lamps outside. This meant there was an air space between the door bottom and the wooden floor.

Billy thought hard for a moment and then dragged himself to Mike's side. "Does that vinegar in the jug have a strong smell?" he asked the cook.

Mike stared at him in surprise. Billy laughed. "I know my question seems crazy, Mike. But I have an idea that might work. Does the vinegar have a strong smell?"

The cook nodded, wrinkling his nose.

"That is all I wanted to know," Billy said. "Here goes, and I hope it works."

He rolled and twisted across the floor until he reached the barrel. Once there, Billy battered himself against the barrel. It rocked back and forth. The vinegar jug swayed but did not fall. Billy braced himself and hit the barrel again. This time, the jug came tumbling off. It hit the floor with a smash.

A flood of vinegar spilled over the floor and streamed through the air space under the door. Billy could hear it splashing like a small waterfall. The sharp smell of the vinegar made him cough; he tried to move away, but he had reached the end of his strength. He rolled over, too weak to move. His eyes watered and every breath of air seemed to burn his lungs.

"If anybody is coming to help us, he had better get here fast," Billy thought.

10

SEA HUNT

Billy drifted as in a dream. The sharp vinegar odor fouled the frigid air of the ice box. How long this went on, Billy could not know. It might have been hours—or merely minutes.

All at once the great door yawned open. Billy raised his head and saw that the doorway was crowded with sailors. Through a mist, he saw Captain Worden push his way inside.

"Get him out of here," he ordered.

Strong hands lifted Billy and carried him out of the ice box. "Mike?" he whispered. "Is Mike all right?"

"Don't worry about him, kid. He is being cared for," a sailor told Billy.

The sailors untied Billy and helped him to the sick

bay, where the *Monitor's* doctor, Lieutenant Dan Ferguson, looked him over carefully.

"I am fine, Lieutenant," he protested. "It is Mike Durgan who needs looking after!"

"The devil I do," roared a voice from the doorway.

Billy turned to see Mike being supported by two sailors, a bandage around his head. "Mike!" he cried and made a move toward the cook.

"Sit down," Lieutenant Ferguson growled. "I am not finished."

"Sorry, sir," Billy said. "I didn't mean . . ."

The doctor tapped Billy on the chest with his finger. "You are as sound as a dollar, my boy, although for the life of me I can't see how that can be. You have been locked in the ice box for hours." He peered at Mike through his silver-rimmed eye glasses. "You are not any the worse either," he told the cook, "except for that knock on your head."

"I am feeling great, sir. All I want is a chance at the birds who tried to do me and Billy in." He held up his fists. "Five minutes alone with them, that's all I want!"

Tom Hurst walked into the sick bay. "I am afraid you will have a long wait, Mike."

"You mean they got away?"

"Clean as a whistle. Those two skunks lowered a boat and took off," Tom said.

"Golly! That is exactly how they said things would work," Billy exclaimed.

"Captain Worden sent me to see how you were," Tom said. "He wants you to report to the officers' room when ready."

"I am ready right now," Mike said.

"Me, too," Billy chimed in.

"Then, let's go," Tom smiled. His face suddenly grew serious as they walked out of the sick bay to the officers' room. "We don't know any more about those two men than we did before."

"That is not quite the case, Lieutenant," Mike said.

Tom looked at him eagerly. "Then, you found out something?"

"Aye. Remember Jed Cudahy, sir?"

"Cudahy!" Tom cried. "Of course I remember him. Why shouldn't I? He was the first man to whom I ever had to give a prison sentence."

"For stealing, it was. A thief on the old *Biscayne Bay!* Enough to break a man's heart. And him the son of a Navy captain," Mike recalled.

"It was a bad business," Tom said. "But what does Cudahy have to do with this?"

"He is the tattooed man! Aye, Jed Cudahy. The fourth man that night in Charleston, when the other lads went to the tattooing parlor with me," Mike cried, stroking his mustache. "And it is Cudahy who has tried to wreck the *Monitor.*"

"Are you sure, Mike?"

The cook touched the bandage on his head. "If you

are thinking this bump rattled my brains, you had best stop, sir. I am not talking wild. Ask young Billy."

"He is right, Tom. Cudahy is the man, just as Mike says," Billy said.

They had reached the officers' room by this time. "Let's save the rest of it for Captain Worden," Tom said, motioning for Billy and Mike to enter the room.

Captain Worden rose from his chair and smiled at Billy. "I have had a long wait for my coffee, lad."

"Aye, sir," Billy laughed. "So have I. A mighty cold wait, too."

"And how are you, Durgan?" the Captain asked the cook.

"Oh, fine, sir. Fine. They dented my head a bit, but I am none the worse," Mike said. "Except for one thing . . ."

"What is that?" Captain Worden asked.

"I will never feel the same about using vinegar again —even in a salad dressing," Mike grinned. "Phew! The smell of it!"

"If it had not been for that vinegar odor, you and Billy might be frozen solid. We could smell the stuff all the way up on deck," Captain Worden said.

"It was Billy's idea to knock over the vinegar jug," Mike said. "He is a smart lad!"

"That he is," Captain Worden declared. "But handing out compliments is not my purpose. Exactly what happened, Durgan? I want the whole story."

Mike told how he had been working in the kitchen when he was struck on the head from behind and how he woke up in the ice box with Billy tied up beside him.

"But most important, sir, I know one of the men. I shipped with him on the *Biscayne Bay*," Mike said. "And so did Lieutenant Hurst."

"What?" Worden exclaimed. "A Navy man?"

"I believe you know him, too, sir," Tom said. "His name is Jed Cudahy."

"Cudahy! Captain Asa Cudahy's son? Of course I know him. He went bad after that sentence he was given on the *Biscayne Bay*. You were the officer who made the charges against him, weren't you, Hurst?"

"Aye, sir," Tom said. "Jed Cudahy was caught stealing money from a shipmate. I happened to be duty officer and arrested him."

"As I recall, he broke out and disappeared. His poor father died soon after. Asa had pinned great hopes on that boy." Worden sighed and shook his head. "Jed was a wild young man. In '57, he was dismissed from the Naval Academy for breaking orders. Asa thought that a hitch in the regular Navy would set him right—but it did not do any good."

"That is the man," Tom said. "This time, he has done a lot worse than steal a few dollars."

"Aye. At least we are not stabbing in the dark. We know the man. Any information on the fellow with him?" Captain Worden asked.

"His name is Wes, sir. At least that is what Cudahy called him," Billy said.

"There is nothing more we can do right now," the Captain said. "Both of them made a clean escape. As soon as possible, I will have all authorities warned by telegraph. Meanwhile, gentlemen, there is a lot of hard work to do. We may very likely have to fight a battle in the morning."

"Aye, sir. What are your orders?" Tom asked.

"All hands will remain at battle stations until further orders."

"Aye, sir."

"What is the latest word from the gun tower?"

"All clear for action, Captain. The guns are clean and everything is in first-class order," Tom reported.

"Good. Report to me later in the wheel house," Captain Worden said. "And by the way, Lieutenant—standing to battle stations all night is not easy. See that the men are made as comfortable as possible. I want them to have plenty of hot coffee and an extra portion of rum."

"Thank you, sir. I will see to it," Tom said.

Captain Worden walked out with firm steps. His face was troubled. In a few hours, the *Monitor* would be in a fight that could decide the future of the United States.

When the Captain left, Tom spoke to Billy and Mike. "I will need every hand I can round up. Are you two feeling fit enough for duty?"

"Now, what kind of a question is that, Lieutenant?

Do you think a little tap on the head is enough to stop Mike Durgan! Of course I am fit for duty—and I will speak for Billy, too! Right, lad?"

"Right! Really, Tom, just tell us what to do," Billy said.

"You go along with Mike. He will have plenty of work for you. Lots of coffee, Mike! And keep it coming," Tom warned.

"I will do better than coffee," the cook promised. "There will be plenty of hot biscuits, too. You would think this was the first time Mike Durgan stood to battle stations all night. Why, when I was on the old *Hartford* in the Mexican War, we . . ."

Tom threw up his hands. "Please, Mike, spare us that story. It is different every time you tell it."

Mike tugged at his mustache. "Ah, you surprise me, Lieutenant, worrying about facts, which only spoil a good story. Come on, Billy. I will finish the yarn while we get the biscuits ready."

"Don't let him fill your head with his tales, Billy!" Tom called after them, with a laugh.

That night, Billy made himself useful in many ways. He served coffee to the men at their posts. When that was finished, he filled shells with powder, cut fuses, loaded bullet cases, did the many tasks in preparation for a battle at sea.

At daybreak, Billy was serving coffee again, this time

to the men on duty in the wheel house. Tom was the officer on watch, and he stood looking at the ocean through a pair of powerful Navy glasses.

Billy moved among the men in the wheel house, serving mugs of coffee from the big tray he carried. He brought a last cup to Tom, who accepted it with thanks.

"Now, that hits the spot," Tom said, sipping the coffee. He had set down his glasses on a small shelf. Billy peered out through an opening in the wheel house's armor. The rising sun cast a red glow on the smooth water. Morning mist was slowly lifting and, even without glasses, Billy could see far off where sea and sky meet.

Suddenly, a shout came from the sailor on watch in the crow's nest, "Three ships dead ahead!"

Tom grabbed his glasses and looked at the distant ships. "They are flying Old Glory," he said. "Must be part of our fleet off Norfolk."

"Are we that close to shore?" Billy asked.

"Land ho!" the sailor called.

"There is your answer, lad!" Tom said. He lowered the glasses. "I am glad to see those ships—it means the *Merrimack* has not finished all of them."

"Golly, I hadn't thought of that," Billy said. "May I have a look?"

"Of course," Tom said, handing him the glasses.

Billy watched the ships for a few moments. He could make out the men at the deck guns and saw others moving about. There were three Union vessels and, from the sails that were raised, Billy could tell the ships had been cleared for action.

As the *Monitor* approached, signal flags were raised on all three vessels. The signal man on duty in the wheel house read the message: "Welcome, *Monitor!*" Billy then turned from the ships and looked out toward the open sea beyond.

Suddenly a sail came into sight. The vessel was cutting through the water. As he watched her, Billy noticed the boat was flying no flag and, when she came closer, he saw a man in a U. S. Navy uniform handling the wheel.

Apparently, because she sat so low in the water, the *Monitor* had not yet been seen by anyone aboard the other boat. Billy turned his glasses on the man at the wheel. He was certainly wearing a Navy uniform. Yet the ship was not a naval craft.

Very excited, Billy called Tom's attention to the boat and gave him the glasses. After a few moments, Tom said, "You are right, Billy. There is something strange about that vessel. Why isn't she flying any colors? I am going to have a closer look."

An order from Tom sent the *Monitor* steaming across the boat's path. Tom kept watching the sleek sailing ship.

"They have seen us now! They are changing course!" Tom turned to the signal man. "Signal her to stop!"

"Aye, sir!" Moments later, a red light rose from the *Monitor* and flashed across the sky, passing directly over the boat.

That swift craft turned from the iron ship and started to race away. Tom reached for the speaking tube.

"Gun tower! Fire a round across the bow of that boat."

Billy watched as the gun boomed and, moments later, a great splash showed where the shell had landed in the water just in front of the boat.

Captain Worden came running into the wheel house, tugging at his sword belt. "What are you shooting at, Lieutenant?" he demanded.

115

Tom quickly told him about the boat. Worden lifted his glasses and looked at the fleeing vessel. "Refused to halt for a signal light and a shot across the bow, eh? I will have her stopped!"

The Captain picked up the speaking tube. "Fire directly to hit!" he ordered.

The blast of the eleven-inch gun made the *Monitor* shiver from stem to stern. A second shot followed moments later and splintered the forward part of the boat.

"Great shooting!" Captain Worden shouted.

A third shell struck the boat in the middle. Flame leaped up from the shattered vessel. Billy gulped when the smoke cleared away. The sleek boat had become a floating ruin. He had never before seen the result of cannon fire.

Men appeared on the deck of the wrecked boat. Billy watched them leaping into the water, fighting to cling to floating pieces of the ship.

"Put about to pick up any men still alive," Captain Worden ordered. When the ship had changed course, the Captain turned to Tom. "Have a boat ready. Get the wounded in first."

"Aye, sir," Tom saluted.

Billy swallowed hard and went to Captain Worden. "Sir, may I go with Lieutenant Hurst? I want to help."

"Go ahead, lad," Worden said. "You may as well see the real face of war—the dead, the wounded and the frightened. Go ahead. Take a close look at what an eleven-inch shell can do to men and ships!"

"Yes, sir," Billy said.

He sat silently in the bow of the boat as six big crew men pulled on the oars. Two sailors with guns were in the bow. He shared a seat with Tom.

"What's the matter, Billy?" Tom asked. "Are you losing your taste for action?"

"Yes, Tom," Billy murmured. "It was awful to see that beautiful ship blown apart, just awful."

117

"That is not the worst, my boy. Remember, there were men on that ship. But you must also remember that this is war and we must do whatever must be done or the enemy will destroy us!"

"I understand, Tom," Billy said, shaking his head, "but I don't like it."

He peered out over the side of the boat as they reached the area where the sailors were trying to keep their heads above water. A sharp piece of mast came drifting by with a sailor clinging to it. Billy saw him let go and slip into the water. A crimson trail floated after the man.

"He's hurt!" Billy shouted. "I am going in after him!"

Pausing only to pull off his shoes, Billy dived in, paying no attention to Tom's shout. He saw the man floating limply and, reaching him, grabbed his right wrist.

Then he saw the rearing-horse tattoo mark on the back of the man's hand.

11

THE BATTLE

Billy was a strong swimmer, and he kept the man's head above water until they came to a piece of the wrecked boat. Billy clung to this with one arm and to Jed Cudahy with the other. The *Monitor* was steaming in a wide circle. On her deck were men of the crew who tossed lines to those in the water to haul them aboard. Meanwhile, Tom Hurst's boat was picking up as many other men as could be found.

As Billy watched, the splintered boat suddenly heeled over and turned bottom side up. Within moments, she slid beneath the water, disappearing in a whirl of foam.

The lifeboat headed in Billy's direction. A sailor tossed him a line, which he tied around his prisoner. Minutes later, both were in the boat, heading for the *Monitor*.

Three sailors from the wrecked boat sat in the bow staring at the *Monitor* sailors, who guarded them with rifles. Jed Cudahy had been placed on a seat in the stern. Tom and Billy bent over him. The tattooed man's Navy blouse was stained with blood and a crimson stream flowed from a wound in his right shoulder.

"We will have to stop that bleeding," Tom muttered. He reached under the seat and found a medical kit, a box which contained bandages. Quickly, he dressed the wound and then looked up at Billy.

"That will hold him until the doctor can treat his shoulder. He caught a piece of shell in it."

"Will he—will he die?" Billy asked.

Tom shook his head. "Not from this wound. He will live to hang for what he has done."

Cudahy soon stirred, groaned, and opened his eyes. He glared at Tom and Billy with hate. "Well, it is the high and mighty Lieutenant Hurst and his young friend," Cudahy said weakly.

"Look, mister, better mind your tongue. You are in enough hot water," Tom warned.

"You don't bother me, even a little," Cudahy said. Sitting up, he held firmly his injured shoulder. "Maybe it doesn't look so good for me right now—but things will change. Right quick, too, once the *Merrimack* gets to work on that tin-can ship of yours."

"All right, that's enough, Cudahy. Where is your partner?" Tom said.

"I don't know. Dead maybe. You blasted us hard," the prisoner said. "And save your breath, Hurst, I am not answering any questions."

"We will see about that," Tom declared. The lifeboat was approaching the *Monitor*. Cupping his hands around his mouth, Tom called to the sailors on the ship. "Prepare to take prisoners on board. One wounded man."

"Aye, sir," one of the crew shouted.

Soon everyone was safely back on board. Nine men had been saved from the boat; Cudahy was the only one wounded and, according to the prisoners, three or four men were missing. After questioning the men, Captain Worden learned that the boat had belonged to the Rebels. She was the *Thetis*, which was on a duty kept secret from the crew. The captain and first mate of the *Thetis* were among the missing. Since nothing further could be discovered from the men, Captain Worden ordered that dry clothing be given them. Officer Ed Healey marched them off to be locked up in the brig.

Tom and Billy were called to the officers' room. Captain Worden was there, pacing the floor. "I am about to question Jed Cudahy," he said, "and I want both of you here when I do so. I just had word from Lieutenant Ferguson in the sick bay that the prisoner's wound is not serious. They will be bringing him up here any moment."

The swinging doors opened and Cudahy came in. Two sailors with big Navy Colt pistols at their hips were on either side of him. The tattooed man's right arm was in a sling.

"Wait outside," Captain Worden told them. The guards saluted and left the room, posting themselves at the door. "Sit down, Cudahy," the Monitor's Captain said, pointing to a chair.

"I will stand if you don't mind," Jed said. "Now let's cut short all this nonsense. I am not going to tell you anything."

Captain Worden smiled. "This will come as a surprise to each of you—and most especially to Mr. Cudahy—but there is not much I need you to tell me." He walked to his desk and took out an oilskin case, which he opened. Inside was a leather notebook. "This, as you can see, was kept in a waterproof case . . ."

"What has that got to do with me?" Cudahy said. "It is not mine."

"No, that is true. One of the boat's crew had it on his person. He happened to snatch it up when the ship was hit. The poor fellow thought he was grabbing a bag of money. When he was taken from the water, we found the case and its contents."

"Listen, Captain, I don't give a hoot. Is that plain enough? I will tell you nothing," Cudahy said.

"Ah, that is just it. All that I need to put a rope around your neck is in this book. You see, it belonged to your partner, Wes Cummings. He had a strange need to write down everything." Captain Worden leafed through the book. "It is all here, Mr. Cudahy: how you offered your services to the Rebels and were given special duty behind our lines." The Captain turned over the pages and then said, "Now, here he tells how you were sent with him to destroy the *Monitor* . . ."

"I don't want to hear any more," Cudahy snapped. "Wes never had any brains. I am glad he drowned. The fool!"

Captain Worden tapped the book. "There is enough in here to hang you."

"What of it?" the prisoner shouted. "You think I am scared? I don't care what happens to me, but I will live long enough to see the United States Navy smashed to bits! And that suits me fine!"

"Cudahy, I knew your father. We served together on several ships. For his sake, don't make matters worse," Captain Worden said.

"Look, you have what you want. Let me alone," Cudahy said. "I have reasons for what I did. I was tossed out of the U. S. Navy—ask Lieutenant Hurst about that—and I swore I would get even. Well, no matter what happens to me, you are all doomed, too!"

"I have had enough," Captain Worden said. "Call in the guards, Lieutenant, and see that he is locked safely away."

Tom stepped to the door and spoke to the guards, who came in and placed themselves on either side of the prisoner. "Take him away, Lieutenant," Worden ordered.

Before Tom could move, Cudahy suddenly rushed at the guard on his right. Reaching across with his good hand, the prisoner pulled the sailor's pistol from its case. The second guard went to grab him, but Cudahy fired from the hip, dropping the man. Keeping the weapon on Tom, Billy and Captain Worden, he picked up the little book with his right hand, grunting with pain as he moved the arm.

He then backed out the door. "I will kill the first man who makes a move," he said. Pausing in the doorway, he turned his head to glance out into the hall. In that second, Billy leaped to the Captain's desk and picked

up a glass paper weight, throwing it at Cudahy in almost a single motion. The tattooed man swung his pistol at Billy and fired just as the weight struck his forehead.

Billy heard the bullet whistle by his ear and strike the wall. He saw the paper weight hit Cudahy. The prisoner staggered a few steps and then dropped. At that moment, steps pounded down the passage. Sailors with drawn revolvers came on the run. Cudahy rose slowly to his feet, staring into the circle of guns that surrounded him.

"Off to the brig with the prisoner!" Captain Worden roared. "Put him in irons and under double guard."

A sailor picked up the little book and handed it to the Captain. "He must have dropped this, sir."

"Thanks, lad," Worden said, taking the book.

The guard who had been wounded by Cudahy's shot was carried out to the sick bay. Then the Captain turned to Billy, who stood white-faced near him. "That was quick thinking, boy. But it was a foolish move. Cudahy would not have gone far. But you were very brave. I don't forget brave deeds."

"I did what I could, sir," Billy said.

"It was plenty," Tom said.

Captain Worden went up to the wheel house and Tom reported to the gun tower, where the men remained at battle stations. A strange calm settled on the *Monitor* as she slowly steamed to join the wooden ships at anchor off Hampton Roads.

Billy went up on deck and stood in the shadow of the

gun tower, staring out over the stretch of water that separated the *Monitor* from the other vessels in the fleet.

The sun had come up and shone from a clear sky. Its rays made dancing ripples of light on the glass-smooth water. From where he stood, Billy could make out the distant shore line, the dark clumps of trees beyond the sandy white beach. He saw the buildings like toy houses against a background of green.

The weather was warm, the breezes gentle. There was more than a hint of spring's arrival on this pleasant March morning. Billy found it hard to believe that he was not on a pleasure trip but a trip which could only end in some death, injury and sunken ships for both sides.

The three big wooden ships swayed slightly as they rode the soft waves. They seemed to be decorated for a holiday with bright pennants fluttering from their masts. The bright flags, Billy knew, were signal flags by which the ships talked with each other. The sunlight caught the barrel of a cannon on one of the wooden ships and Billy saw the flash as the light hit against the polished metal.

He leaned on the railing, drinking in the sights. Somehow, it did not seem real that men were preparing to kill one another on such a day. His chain of thought was stopped by the boom of a cannon which sounded across the water.

The shot had come from the most distant of the three wooden vessels. A cloud of gray-white gun smoke rose over the ship and hung like a veil around the masts.

The first shot was followed by another. Now there was a burst of activity aboard the three Union ships. Sails were raised and the craft swung around toward the open sea. They went beyond the *Monitor* so that the iron ship stood between them and the shore line.

Signal men were busy sending messages to the *Monitor*. Captain Worden appeared at the wheel house door.

"Sound general quarters! All hands to battle stations!"

A sailor with a bugle blew the call. Once again sailors dashed to their battle posts and stood awaiting orders.

Thus far, nobody had seen the mark at which the wooden ship had been firing. Morning mists still were rising near the shore and formed a curtain. All eyes peered in the direction toward which the firing had been aimed.

Suddenly, a cry ran through the *Monitor* as the mist parted and the *Merrimack* broke through the opening into the sunlight.

Billy stepped back from the railing to look at the monster of a ship. He had once seen a picture of a huge beast, and the giant *Merrimack* reminded him of that creature.

She rode in the water, like a barn floating out to sea with black cannon poking out of firing ports. Her iron sides were like a giant's armor. Attached to her bow was a long iron ram pointed into a sharp beak which could cut into the strongest timber on a ship.

The construction of the
Merrimack

Beside this huge vessel, the *Monitor* seemed very small. "It is David and Goliath all over again!" Billy thought.

"Everybody take cover!" Captain Worden bellowed. "You, Billy Harper! Report to Lieutenant Hurst in the tower and make yourself useful. Men, we shall close with the enemy soon! Stick to your guns, do your duty, trust in God and the right of our cause! Good luck, all hands!"

Billy dashed along the deck to the tower. A moment later he was inside. The crew stood stripped to the waist peering out of the firing slits at the *Merrimack*.

"Big, isn't she?" one said.

"Makes her easy to hit," another man replied.

"Stop that talk," a third snapped. "It is going to be a tough scrap."

Billy went to Tom Hurst, who was peering through the sights of No. 1 gun. "Captain told me to report here," he said.

"There will be plenty of work," Tom said. He slapped a crew member on the back. "There you are, Tompkins. Dead center. You will score a direct hit."

Tom spoke to each of the men in the gun crews. He offered advice and help. "The main thing is to keep calm, boys. Remember, the Rebels are as scared as we are!" He laughed and the men joined him.

The two ships circled each other carefully. Billy found a peephole and stayed there, watching the *Merrimack's* moves. It seemed hours that the two iron ships circled without a shot being fired by either one of them. Once in a while, from long range, one of the wooden ships in the Union fleet would fire on the Southern ship but without making a dent.

Suddenly, the *Merrimack* let loose with a burst from five guns at about seven hundred yards.

The shells struck the *Monitor's* tower. There was a crash and a ringing of metal. Billy thought his eardrums would burst from the sound. The force of the heavy shells shook the tower, and anyone near the walls was knocked from his feet. Billy went flying head over heels, but picked himself up at once. Gun smoke filled the tower and bits of bursting shell rained down on the iron roof like hail.

"Anybody hurt?" Tom yelled.

"No, sir!" a voice answered.

"All right, then. They have started the ball. Let's show them we can hit, too! Number 1 gun! Fire!"

The blast swept a wave of furnace heat into the tower. Billy turned his face away and gulped. But before he had recovered, Tom yelled, "Number 2 gun! Fire!"

Again the report shook Billy. But all at once he was too busy to think of the heat, the exploding shells, the sharp odor of gun powder. He was carrying buckets of water to the men, helping bring shells to the guns, carrying bags of powder.

Again and again, the *Merrimack's* shells smashed against the tower without damage. The battle went on and on. The sun rose higher, and inside the tower it grew hotter.

During a rest in the fighting, Billy sat on the floor. Tom grinned at him, his face smeared with gun powder stains.

"How is it going, lad?" Tom asked.

"Great," Billy said. "Just great. I couldn't feel hotter, more tired or dirtier."

"That's war." Tom laughed.

Then a frightened voice shouted, "Lieutenant! Lieutenant! The Merrimack is getting ready to ram us!"

Everyone dashed to a firing slit or a peep hole. Billy stared in horror as the huge bulk of the Merrimack came toward the tiny Monitor—and the great, sharp ram seemed aimed straight at him.

12

A DREAM COME TRUE

The men in the tower stood rooted to the spot as the *Merrimack* bore down on the *Monitor;* there seemed to be nothing that could stop the giant speeding at them.

Tom leaped to the speaking tube which connected with the wheel house. "*Merrimack* is going to ram!"

"We see her!" Captain Worden replied. "Stand fast for a sudden turn."

Just as the Rebel ship's ram was about to touch the *Monitor,* the little ship turned off and the clumsy *Merrimack* lumbered past. A rain of bullets rattled off her sides, for the men on the *Monitor* hoped to shoot the *Merrimack's* men through the firing ports.

But that was a vain hope. The rifle shots bounced against the iron ship's armor like dried peas on a tin roof. As she swept by the *Monitor,* the enemy vessel fired from her stern guns.

One shell exploded with tremendous force at the No. 1 gun-firing slit. The shock knocked down every man on the gun crew. Billy was flung against a wall so hard that his nose began to bleed. Tom was thrown to the floor.

Billy shook his head and wiped the blood from his nose with the back of his hand. He stepped over the men of the gun crew and went to the loaded cannon. He was fighting mad.

The chief gunner was trying to get up, and Billy helped him to his feet. The man's left arm was badly hurt. But Billy wanted to strike at the Rebels, and the only way to do that was by shooting back. No. 2 gun was out of position, and by the time the tower could be revolved, the *Merrimack* would no longer be there.

Billy asked the chief gunner to sight the big gun for him, then he peered through the sight as he had seen the others do. The cannon was sighted straight on the *Merrimack.*

"One! Two! Three!" Billy shouted. He pulled the heavy cord. The gun leaped as though it were alive. Smoke rose up into the tower and the cannon slid back along its tracks. The big eleven-inch gun had scored a direct hit on the *Merrimack.* Billy let out a yell as he saw pieces of wood and metal fly up into the air.

"We hit her! We hit her!" he cried.

Men from the No. 2 gun crowded around to see.

"You got her, lad!" one of the sailors exclaimed.

"Good boy!" another said, clapping Billy on the back. Billy turned to congratulate the chief gunner.

Bleeding from a slight head cut, Tom dragged himself to the firing slit. He grinned back at Billy. "You two hit the only spot on the *Merrimack* that could hurt her," Tom told Billy. "The shell damaged the rudder," he went on. Now Billy understood why the crew was so excited. The rudder was the heavy, weighted fin by which the ship was steered. "They won't be able to steer well enough to give us trouble now. Good shooting, lad. Good shooting."

The praise that was showered on Billy and the chief gunner was halted when Captain Worden called the tower on the speaking tube.

"Who fired that shot?" he asked.

"It was Billy Harper, sir," Tom replied.

"Send him to the wheel house. I want to shake his hand," the Captain said.

A few minutes later, Billy stood by Captain Worden in the wheel house.

As smiling officers looked on, the Captain ruffled the boy's hair.

"We are proud of you, son," he said. "You are a real Navy man!"

"Thank you, sir," Billy smiled, his heart swelling with happiness. "But the chief gunner sighted her for me, sir."

An officer watching the *Merrimack* which was slowly steaming along about five hundred yards away, announced, "I think she is pulling out, sir. She has had enough!"

Worden stepped to a slit and peered through it. "She is hurt, all right, but far from finished. I know her Captain, Franklin Buchanan. He will put that rudder in working order if it is at all possible. This fight is not over."

Before he could pull his face away from the slit, there

was the sound of something exploding. Orange flame and black smoke stabbed from the *Merrimack's* guns.

The sound of shells tore the air and was followed moments later by rocking crashes that shook the wheel house. With ear-splitting noise and shattering blasts, bursting shells smashed into the wheel house and knocked every man there to the floor.

The crew man managed to grip the wheel, so the *Monitor* held her course. But for a moment, the ship was without any control; every officer lay on the floor.

Billy rose slowly to his knees, shaking his head from side to side, trying to clear his thoughts. One by one, the officers stirred and drew themselves erect. Captain Worden sat with his face in his hands, rocking slightly from side to side.

Billy jumped to him. "Are you all right, sir?" he asked.

"Help me up," Worden whispered.

Several officers pulled him to his feet. Worden dropped his hands from his face and stared blankly about the wheel house.

"I can't see," he exclaimed. "I am blind."

"No! No!" an officer cried.

"I can't see," Worden repeated. "There was a great flash before my eyes; then I was knocked down."

"I will get Lieutenant Ferguson," Billy said. He rushed out of the wheel house to the sick bay, returning with the doctor minutes later.

As Ferguson examined the Captain, the gun duel went

on. The *Monitor's* guns continued to fire, scoring hit after hit on the *Merrimack*. But even the hard-hitting guns could not dent the enemy's armor. The eleven-inch shells shook up the *Merrimack's* crew. It appeared that a few men were wounded by shell splinters, but nothing the *Monitor* did could really hurt the Rebel ship.

Nor could the larger *Merrimack* make the tiny *Monitor* quit. The sturdy craft took the best the Rebels had without giving in.

The worst thing that happened on the *Monitor* was the injury to Captain Worden. The officers in the wheel house stood with grim and sober faces while Lieutenant Ferguson peered into Worden's eyes.

At last the doctor stood up. "I don't think the damage will remain. I will have to put a bandage across your eyes, sir. The powder flash injured a nerve. I believe the damage will last only for short time."

"Blind," Captain Worden whispered. "I am blind!"

"Please, sir, don't . . ." the doctor said.

"Never mind, Ferguson. Save your speeches. Whether I can see or not, we are in battle. Have Lieutenant Hurst come here from the tower. Tell him to take over and to keep driving until we win or go under," Worden said.

"The speaking tube is out," an officer said. "That last hit must have done it."

"I will go for Tom," Billy cried.

He ran to the tower and, in the noise and racket of

the battle, told Tom what had happened. Soon Tom took over Captain Worden's place in the wheel house. The doctor had the Captain carried below, where he could better examine the injury.

It seemed to Billy that the fight had gone on for days without stopping. But, at last, it was sunset and the fierce battle began to die down. Both ships were still alive, the men dead on their feet, neither crew able to finish off the other. As the evening shadows were closing in, the *Merrimack* finally turned and limped away, back to her port. The field was left to the *Monitor* and, while it was not a clear-cut victory, at least the small iron ship had proved that she could stand off the big Rebel ship that had threatened to sink the entire Union Navy.

Tired sailors fell asleep at their posts. Billy stayed at Tom's side in the wheel house as the *Monitor* steamed slowly back and forth across the line of wooden ships she was guarding like a sheep dog.

Tom remained on duty all that night, but the strain was too much for Billy, who curled up in a corner of the wheel house and fell into a deep sleep. The next day, he awakened with a sense of pride and pleasure that he had been part of the great battle.

There was good news from the sick bay about Captain Worden. His eyes were not badly hurt. In time, his sight would return, but for many months he would have to wear special eye glasses.

Captain Worden was taken from the *Monitor* and

sent aboard one of the wooden ships, to a hospital in Washington. The same vessel carried Jed Cudahy—under heavy guard and wearing hand and leg irons—to a naval prison near the capital, where he would stand trial. The other prisoners were also sent to a prison camp.

The *Monitor*, now under Tom Hurst's command, remained on duty at Hampton Roads for several weeks. Tom did not receive orders to bring the *Monitor* back to the Brooklyn Navy Yard until soldiers from the Union Army captured the port of Norfolk and the *Merrimack* was blown up by the Southern soldiers before they left the port.

Billy Harper knew he would never forget the way the

Monitor was greeted when the ship returned to the Navy Yard.

Bands were playing and crowds of sailors and others lined the shore as the *Monitor*, with victory flags flying, steamed slowly to the dock. Wives, sweethearts and parents were waiting for the crew men when they came on shore.

Billy went down to the dock, smiling a little sadly as the sailors were greeted by their loved ones. He felt lonely and wished someone were there to greet him.

Suddenly, he heard his name being called. Looking up, he saw Mr. and Mrs. Dobbins rushing toward him.

"Oh, Billy, Billy!" Mollie Dobbins wept as she clasped him to her. "Oh, Billy!"

Fred Dobbins stood grinning, with tears shining in his eyes. He took Billy's hand. "We are glad to have you back, son."

And where he had been almost unhappy before, not feeling wanted, belonging to no one, Billy now knew that the Dobbinses had a place in their hearts for him.

Mollie Dobbins wiped her eyes. She stepped back and looked at Billy.

"Did they not feed you on that vessel?" she scolded. "You are as thin as a starved sparrow. It's off to home, now. I will put some flesh on your bones!"

"Ah, Billy, if you think the Rebel shot and shell was fierce, you will now be facing real thunder," Fred Dobbins said. "My Mollie is that terrible when she has a cause—and right now her cause is to make you gain a little weight!"

"Hush up, Fred!" Mollie said. "It is enough to break a body's heart the way the poor lad looks. Come along, come along at once!"

Fred winked at Billy and the two followed Mrs. Dobbins.

Some weeks later, on a day in early June, Billy was standing at the Navy Yard gate with his shoe-shine box when a sailor came up to him.

"Hey, Billy, they want you up at Yard headquarters," the sailor said.

"Me?"

"That's what Captain Worden said. 'Fetch Billy Harper,' he told me."

Billy packed up his kit, left it at the guard's booth and went with the messenger. In the vine-covered headquarters building, he was greeted by Tom Hurst and Captain Worden. Except for the eye glasses, he was just the same as Billy had first known him. He showed no other signs of his late injury.

"Billy, come along with me," the Captain said. "We have to go see Commander Paulding. I want you to come, too, Lieutenant Hurst."

They all went into Commander Paulding's office. The gray-haired, fierce-eyed officer was seated behind his desk.

After greeting Tom and Captain Worden, he turned

his stern gaze on Billy. "So this is the lad, eh?" he asked.

"Aye, sir," Captain Worden replied.

"I have been told that you want to be a Navy man, son," Commander Paulding said to Billy.

"Yes, sir," the boy replied. "I want to join up more than anything. But I can't, at least not for a while. I am too young by a year, sir. But I plan to join the Navy as soon as I can, sir."

"It is true that you are too young for the regular Navy. But, if you really want to be a United States Navy man, I think something might be arranged."

"What?" Billy cried. "Is there a chance that I can join the Navy now?"

"Whoa! Hold your horses, lad," Commander Paulding laughed. "I never said that. However, I think you are Navy material and, according to Captain Worden and Lieutenant Hurst, you are a real fighting wildcat."

"Make that a couple of wildcats," Captain Worden grinned.

Paulding reached into his desk and took out an official-looking paper. "Billy," he said, "this is a special order from the Secretary of the Navy appointing you a midshipman at the U. S. Naval Academy to reward you for services aboard the *Monitor* and for helping to capture Jed Cudahy."

"Me? A midshipman?" Billy gasped.

"Why, is there anything wrong with that?" Tom Hurst asked.

"No, no, of course not," Billy said. "Oh, golly, Tom! Me, a midshipman!"

"And four years from now, you will be a Navy officer," Tom said.

"It's a dream come true!" Billy whispered.

"Not yet, lad," Paulding smiled. "First, you will have to sign this paper. Then you will have four years of very hard work—harder even than the rest of the boys, for you have missed some of the schooling that they have had. But I have a feeling you are up to it." He smiled at Billy warmly as he held out the pen. Billy took it and signed his name to the paper.

"I am used to hard work," the boy said. "I think I can make it, all right."

"One more thing, Billy," Captain Worden said. "When you graduate from the Academy, I want you to serve on my ship."

"Well, what do you think of that?" Tom asked. "You have a call to duty even before you have gone to your first class!"

"What can I think?" Billy exclaimed, his eyes wide with surprise and pleasure. "I think it is wonderful, just wonderful!"